WHAT MIGHT HAVE BEEN

ELIZABETH JOHNS

PROLOGUE

Vitoria, Spain, June 1813
The Allied Encampment

The grief was so thick in their throats none could speak. They had been together for only two years, yet the bonds of the battle were forged stronger than any created by blood. It was not something that could be explained, only experienced.

When they had set sail from England for the Peninsula, each had felt invincible, ready to conquer evil and save England. Now, it was hard to remember why they needed to be brave anymore.

James shivered. There was a chill in the air as they all sat huddled around the fire. The silence the night before a battle was eerie, but after, it was deafening. Watching the flames perform their blue, gold and orange dance, it did not seem real that one of them was gone. They had survived Ciudad Rodrigo, Badajoz, and Salamanca, yet Peter had fallen before their eyes today. His sabre had been raised and his eyes fierce, ready to charge when a shot had seared through him. He was on his horse one moment and gone the next. The scene replayed over and over in their minds in slow-motion. Memory was a cruel, cruel master. The same battle had left Luke wounded when a shell exploded near him. He insisted on joining them, eschewing the orders of the sawbones and hobbling out of the medic tent on the arm of his batman, Tobin.

Now, there were six of them left, if Peter's widow was included, and all wondered *was this to be their fate?*

Someone had to speak and break the chain of their morbid, damning thoughts.

"Peter would not want this." Five pairs of morose eyes looked up at Matthias. "We all knew this was likely when we signed up to fight Napoleon."

"How would you want us to feel if it were you?" James asked.

"I would want you to keep going forward and give my life meaning."

"Precisely. We mourn this night and move forward tomorrow. His death shall not be in vain." James said with quiet conviction.

"What about Kitty?" Peter's wife that followed the drum and felt like one of them.

"We see what she wishes to do. I expect she will wish to return home," Matthias answered. He had known her and Peter from the cradle, and was most devastated by the loss.

"The French are worn down, this cannot go on much longer," Luke said, though he would be sent home. No one else dared voice such hope.

"We are worn down," James muttered.

Philip, the quiet, thoughtful one spoke. "If anything happens to me, will someone see to my sister? She has no one else."

"I swear it," Colin said, leading the others to do the same.

"*Pietas et honos.*"

Philip nodded, too choked up to speak.

"Loyalty and honour," another swore the oath in English.

They returned to silence, each brooding over what had happened and what was yet to come.

CHAPTER 1

*B*eing poor in a rich man's world was a jest of the worst kind. For years, while in the army, James had largely been able to ignore his fate… mainly with humour. Now, it was time to face that fate.

It had been a year since Waterloo, but he was transported there every time he tried to close his eyes and sleep.

Peter and Colin were gone; Matthias, Kitty, Luke, Philip, and even Tobin had married and moved on and found some level of peace with another. It felt as if the entire world had left him behind.

James hated pity and he hated to be pitied, so he behaved as though nothing was wrong. Yet how did it help?

When he had gone home for a brief visit, after seeing Colin's body returned, the signs of decay and ruination had been everywhere.

The lines on his mother's face told him everything he needed to know. His sisters' gowns were so thin and mended that even he could see it. His father was still the same absent-minded, good-intentioned gentleman farmer he had always been—the Englishman who had married a Scottish lass with an estate as her dowry. But good intentions did not feed his family.

James had left ten years ago because there had been nothing for him there then and there was even less now.

Despite knowing what had to be done, he had allowed himself a few weeks of self-pity. He had returned to Thackeray Close, to the reunion of the brethren for Matthias and Kitty's wedding. It had felt to be the end of the best chapter of his life.

It was not that he hated his family, but more what they represented—what he did not want to become. When things were going poorly, they stayed the course and waited for something to happen. How was that a way to live?

Now, he was beholden to a worse emotion than pity—guilt. He could have stayed and helped all those years ago when he had barely had a beard. Would it have really made a difference? His conscience dared to interject.

Perhaps, and perhaps not.

They had all thought his marrying money would save them. Like a good son, he had promptly fallen in love with the rich young lady in the neighbourhood and had been publicly rejected by her father. He had left as much to escape as to nurse his wounded pride—not that he had been given the choice to stay.

Now he was fully versed in the ways of the world. He had sent every spare coin he had home and hoped his father would somehow find a way to manage the farms and the estate.

Hope was futile.

Thankfully, it was a long ride from Sussex to Scotland, and he did not hurry. There were nothing but drainage ditches and crop rotations in his future. Maybe one day he would be able to travel again if he could manage a good wheat or barley crop—once the roof was repaired, once his two younger sisters were married off, once, once, once. It did not bear thinking on in detail or he would lose hope entirely.

At twenty miles per day, it might take him several months. Every wayside tavern and posting inn was an opportunity to be at his leisure and to delay the inevitable.

He had even offered tenancy to a few old soldiers along the way who had no positions to return to because of their injuries. Would they put in an appearance after he had warned them of the dire condition of the estate and that he could not promise roofs which would not leak? He hoped so.

As he neared the Scottish border, instead of hurrying, he slowed down, which said a great deal about the state of his mind. Should he not be rushing forward towards his home? No, he was not one of those men who was saved in battle by visions of what was waiting for him in his homeland.

Not that he was completely without motive, he reflected. Being spurned by Laird McKiernan had moved him to prove himself worthy in the beginning, then once he had fought his first battle, he scarcely thought of him again. Occasionally, when others would receive letters home from their sweethearts, he might think of Lady Annag and wonder what might have been.

He had heard she had married and had a horde of children. Good for her, he had thought at the time—although it was likely he would not recognize her now. Marriage and babies tended to change even Society's most notable beauties. It gave him some little comfort to imagine her changed... as he was. But he could not afford a wife then and he could not afford one now. He was not sure he would want one if he could. All of his friends had found love-matches which made him both nauseous and envious at the same time. Happy endings only seemed to occur when one had pots of money... or, at least, no debt.

On the last occasion James had checked, there was no end to the debt, but frankly, he had not checked since he had left long ago to join the army. Laird McKiernan had at least helped to purchase his Commission or he would have been an enlisted man and likely dead by now, enlisted or no. However, being an officer had not spared Peter or Colin or many other great men by the world's account.

"I am full of such optimism, Sancho," he said to his horse, the one being that had been with him through everything. He had purchased the Spanish horse when offered a great deal by someone who was returning to England to leave the army.

Sancho was not a beautiful horse, but he was loyal and trustworthy. Indeed, it was another miracle Sancho had survived. Some caval-rymen had half a dozen spare horses, whereas James only had the one. Once, when Sancho had been lame, he'd had to borrow a horse from one of the brethren. James' poverty was not something anyone talked about, but he mentioned it in jest from time to time. That was the thing about one's true friends: they never asked nor made you feel awkward.

Several years before, Waverley had offered them all a business venture, but James had not had enough pounds to spare to feel respectable about joining. He supposed, if worse came to worst, he could ask the Duke for a position. Yet guilt kept him moving forward, even at a snail's pace.

He permitted himself a small sigh. Sancho was all he had now. Hopefully, the estate still had plenty of green grass and clover for Sancho to grow fat and lazy on in his retirement. He had earned it.

"What have I earned, you ask? An excellent question, Sancho. It should have been me who died, not Peter or Colin, who had much more to live for. But God has a sense of humour like that."

James appreciated humour. Not everyone did. On some days it was all he had, besides an uncanny ability to live through battle.

He barely had an outward scratch to show for his efforts. Inside was quite another matter. "But we do not talk about that, do we, Sancho?"

Sancho made a noise of disapproval. James would bet on his life that his horse understood him.

"You may be ugly, but you have wits, Sancho." James leaned forward in the saddle and patted his horse's neck.

He sat back and chuckled when he thought of how he had described the McKiernan girls to his friends. A cross between an Arabian and a Clydesman, then he added that might be an insult to the Clydesman.

It was true that two of the girls had faces that resembled horses, and long necks that also would be better served on an equine, but not Annag; not the one he had fallen for and because of whom had been quickly spurned.

His mother still had hopes of aligning their families and their lands, but James would rather work hard on the farm than martyr himself in such a fashion… at least until the roof fell in and the stones crumbled around him.

When at last he reached Galashiels, he stopped at the meadow between Kiernan Castle and Alchnanny. It looked the same as it had that last summer when he had thought he was invincible; when love was as young and sweet as the heather in the meadow.

He reached the lake at the bottom of the valley, which skirted his family property and the McKiernan estate. He dismounted and allowed Sancho to drink. As he watched the water ripple beneath the horse's mouth, he decided a quick dip would not go amiss. He was not delaying, not one bit.

~

Annag McKiernan Calder was rethinking her decision to return home. Her year of mourning had ended and she had thought living with her husband's family to be difficult… until she returned home.

But where else would she go? She supposed she could take her English son to one of her husband's properties, now her son's, and begin anew, but she would never hear the end of it.

When her husband had died, there was no end to the advice—no, commands—her mother-in-law had given on how things were done; how she thought Annag's son should be brought up. Annag had left on a supposed visit to her family as soon as she could, hoping she might find reprieve there, but her mother and younger sisters—still unmarried—were making her run mad. Thinking to find themselves grand matches, they thought it Annag's duty to bring them out. Annag loved her sisters, and tried to tell them that Society was not everything they made it out to be, but it fell on deaf ears.

Annag had done her duty and married grandly, as her parents had wished, and she had been miserable. There had been a time, during her sixteenth summer, when she had been dazzled by a ginger-haired, hazel-eyed boy from the neighbouring estate. Her father had caught a murmur of their young love and James had gone away with a resounding rejection. He had not been lofty enough for Laird McKiernan's eldest and prettiest daughter; he being only a gentleman farmer's son with an English name. Irrespective of these strictures, her father had married her off to an English lord within weeks.

James had then left for the army and Annag had not seen him again. Despite marrying Lord Calder not long afterwards, Annag had watched for news in the casualty lists whenever she could. His name had only been on lists of honour, bravery and valour. He was a hero.

How silly she was even to think James would remember her! Her first marriage had been a lesson in humility. Even though she had not wanted it, she had tried to make the best of it. She had tried to make her husband love her. But he'd had no purpose for her other than to bear him a son. Once that was done, he had stayed in London with his mistress and left Annag in the country.

How might her life have been had she married James? What a futile exercise in conjecture that question was, she reflected, but on coming back to Scotland, she could not help but think of him.

Every day she had gone on long rides, needing to escape the house, and she had ridden by the meadow where James had first kissed her and promised her his undying love.

Annag was not sure she believed in that kind of love anymore. She had seen a few love matches during her short time in London, and in the papers she had read of unconventional couples such as the Duke and Duchess of Waverley, but most of Annag's experience was not with love.

She ought to be grateful to be a young widow, released from a miserable marriage, but she still did not feel free. Her son had been sent to Eton whilst she was in mourning, which broke her heart completely, but the problem with having an earl for a son was she had little say over his upbringing. The best she could do was to be close to him for visits during holidays. It was a wretched business.

Annag stopped at the meadow and let her horse put its head down to graze. She would have to make a decision soon. It was time to find some meaning in life again.

It was the first time in ages she had been able to relax. Breathing deeply of the scents in the lush meadow, being away from her sisters' never-ending obsession with finding a suitor, Annag found it a relief to be alone, to be hugged and caressed by nature. She closed her eyes and felt the sun on her face, the stream trickling behind her and the sense of the fresh wild flowers and pine trees all around her.

Radford had not smelled comforting to her. The place was dark, cold, and musty in her mind. She knew there were gardens there and occasionally some sun, but it had not felt like it. There she felt trapped —here she felt free. Maybe coming home had not been a mistake after all.

Would her mother and sisters understand if she did not accompany them to London? She did not know if she could bear it.

For now, she did not want to think. She let the burden of her husband's death drift away like the rolling clouds above. She fought the anxiety she held over leaving her son at school—not by her choice, and of the problem she still had to face—the thought of the expectations her mother-in-law, mother and sisters all had of her. Perhaps they were trying to distract her and keep her mind occupied. That was being extremely generous, but she did not have to deal with it today. She allowed herself to drift away into a trance-like slumber where she dreamed of better days.

Annag awoke with a start, disoriented, when something wet and foul-smelling touched the side of her face.

She opened her eyes to see two large brown eyes staring at her whilst their owner chewed the strings of her bonnet. It was not her horse, but whose? And where was her own horse?

Sitting up, she looked around, but could see no human. The horse was still saddled, though, so unless this strange horse had thrown its rider, then he—for it was a gentleman's saddle—must not be too far away.

She watched the odd animal chew away at her ribbons. He was not

9

a pretty horse. One might even call him ugly, with his grizzled mane and odd spots. She gave a half-hearted tug and took back the rest of the bonnet.

"You are a naughty horse," she scolded.

She would have sworn he grinned at her.

"Impudent too, I see. Perhaps you did throw your rider. But where? Should I go and search for him to see if he is injured?"

The horse made a noise that almost sounded like 'if you so please.' Now her wits had become addled, imagining a talking horse.

Nevertheless, she was amused and decided she should make some effort to search for the gentleman. The military saddle was decidedly well cared for and unlike anything she had seen before. It looked as though it had been in several battles. But what would it be doing here?

She stood and smoothed out her dress and replaced her bonnet sans ribbons.

"Where is your master?" she asked the horse, which responded by turning around and walking slowly across the meadow, a sward covered in blankets of purple heather and yellow broom.

Morag was still grazing out in the meadow herself. "Minding her own business as a good horse should," Annag muttered.

She therefore followed the golden horse, looking about her for anyone lying about injured, but could see no one. She was not certain how far she would be willing to follow as she neared the land belonging to Squire Frome.

The horse stopped near the lake, which was high in the spring from the thawing snow. This was the same one that pooled at the bottom of her father's land, where she and her sisters had spent countless days playing with the Frome children.

"Are you leading me here to your master or because you have a fancy for a drink?" Why was she talking to this horse like a human?

He tossed his head towards the lake and then set his lips to the water, sucking loudly.

Annag shrugged in a careless fashion her husband had deplored and began to turn away. At that moment, she heard a splash in the water. A sense of foreboding crept over her and she seemed to freeze like ice where she stood instead of turning and escaping as she ought.

A very male backside emerged from the water to the waist, facing away from her, thank the Lord. Despite no longer looking like a boy, it had to be him.

"James," she whispered. It had to be him out here, surely?

She stepped back behind a convenient bush to hide. She was not yet ready to face him, and especially not like this.

What would he think of her now? And acting the voyeur! No, she most certainly did not want to meet him again like this. Did she want to meet him again at all? The rapid beating of her heart told her what a silly question that was.

CHAPTER 2

With a sensation that he was being watched, James stood and looked around, but who could be there? He shook his head and dived back under the water, relishing the icy cold almost as a cleansing. It was time to start his new life and there was naught like a freezing dip to do it.

Once he had dried off on the bank, he dressed again and then found Sancho grazing nearby. He had taken him back to the stables before he noticed a blue ribbon hanging from the side of his mouth, stuck between two of the animal's large teeth.

"Where did you find that?" he asked Sancho. The horse simply ignored the question. Regardless of the answer, it was too fine a ribbon for Sancho's fodder.

It could have belonged to one of his sisters, he supposed.

"You are not a goat to be stealing whatever takes your fancy, my friend," he chastised sternly.

He jerked the piece from Sancho's teeth and removed both saddle and bridle before rubbing him down. It was a soothing task—and a delaying one as well.

The signs of decay and ruin were all about him, just as they had been before. They had not magically disappeared. The stable roof was falling in. The stone walls around the fields were crumbling. The house roof leaked and had been patched so many times that there was probably no original roof left. Weeds overtook any semblance of garden and vines were so thick up the walls that if they cut them back, the house would surely fall.

Thankfully there was at least a safe, dry place for Sancho.

When he could no longer put off going to the house, he picked up his saddlebags and trudged reluctantly up the gravel path from the stable yard.

There was no one to answer the door, of course. The few servants who remained were all overworked. Docherty, who they still referred to as the butler, also performed the tasks of footman, steward and sometimes kitchen maid. His mother shared the duties of house-keeper along with Cook, and his sisters were also called upon to do tasks beneath their station. If they did not marry soon, they would also be living well beneath their station.

As for his father, he continued to spend his days in his study and shuffle pages around while the estate crumbled around him. James was a man of action and he could not fathom how someone could become so overwhelmed they ceased to function, but it seemed to be the case.

"James? Is that you?" his mother's voice called as he entered.

"Mama. It is." He set down his bags and walked forward to kiss her cheek.

"Why did you not inform us you were coming?"

"I did not know when I would arrive," he answered. "Am I unwelcome?" he teased, though he could see by the creases on her face that she was worried. Her hair had faded from a bright red, and was now a yellowing-grey.

"You are never unwelcome, James. How could you think so? In fact, you are needed here now more than ever."

"I am here to help," he assured her, pulling her into his arms. At first, she was stiff, as though she was trying to keep a wall about her, but then he felt her reserve fail and she dissolved into tears in his arms.

He was not a great comforter and was more inclined to say something out of misplaced humour than not, so he kept quiet for once and rubbed his hand up and down her back in what he hoped was a soothing fashion.

"I do not know what came over me," she said as she pulled away from him and dabbed her eyes with her handkerchief.

He led her to the drawing room and sat next to her on a settee. "Are things so dire now?"

"James, they have been dire for years. I have no notion of what is beyond dire. Desperate? I fear we will lose the estate if something does not change very soon."

James thought there were worse fates, but he did not say so. Perhaps they could sell the house and land and buy something smaller. He would have to look into everything and see. They might not like it, but it was better than waiting until the whole was taken away. Then where would they be? He worried not for himself. Wellington would take him back or he could beg Waverley for a position.

"What of my sisters? Have they any prospects? They were both fetching girls, but there was no bevy of gentleman suitors to be had, not within fifty miles.

"They have been reluctant to leave us. Perhaps you can convince them to go to my sister in Edinburgh. They may then have a small season and might make respectable matches."

James could not but feel guilt. If his sisters stayed behind to work then he would ask some of his friends' wives to help. They would do it without question. However, it would require funds.

"Although, you should know, Elspeth has had her eye on the visiting curate. Unfortunately, curates do not have any more pennies to rub together than we do."

"Unless they find a living." James knew some of his brethren were peers and held livings among their various domains. He could see he needed to spend some time with his sisters. "I will speak with them today and enquire what they wish to do. How is Father?"

His mother did not answer immediately, so he looked over at her face. Her chin was quivering and her face was wrinkled with suppressed pain.

"Mama?"

She shook her head, clearly fighting off tears. "I will not lose control of myself again."

"You have had to be strong for a long time, Mama. Please tell me."

"Your father is not well."

"What is wrong?" he urged.

"He is declining, James. He is here but he is not."

"You are not making sense. What has happened?"

"You will see for yourself, but I would be very surprised if he knows who you are."

"Has he had an apoplexy?"

"I cannot say. It has worsened greatly since your last visit."

His father had always been a bit distant, but perhaps this had been coming on for a long time.

"Why did no one tell me?"

"You had enough to worry about in staying alive. Even though it has been hard having you gone, we are still very proud of what you have done."

James clenched his jaw but he did not deny her words. There was little to be proud of, but it would not make her feel better to disillusion her.

"I suppose I should take a look in on Father, then."

He stood up and kissed her cheek once again before seeking out his father in his study. He was always either there or in the garden tending the bees.

It was with dread that he opened the door to find his father sitting in a chair, a blanket over his knees and staring into the fire.

He walked towards him, and knelt down before him. His father looked into his face, but his mother had been correct—there was no recognition—no Papa looking back at him. Had James missed the signs before or had he simply ignored them in his subconscious?

"How are you, Father?" he asked.

The older gentleman smiled pleasantly. "It is chilly today." He remarked words that he would say to any man, not his only son who he had not seen in some time.

It was not at all cold, but James would not contradict him.

Instead of acknowledging the feel of a knife turning in his chest, he looked at the muddle of paper scattered across the desk and on the floor that had not seen attention in months, if not years.

"Welcome home," he whispered to himself, allowing one last moment of pity.

No one else would indulge him such a luxury. It was time to roll up his sleeves and get to work.

He turned back to his father, who seemed content to stare at the fire. "Would you like anything, Papa?"

His father did not even seem to hear him. James did not know what to say or how to feel, so he left to seek out his sisters. He might as well learn the entire extent of his sins.

He found them both in the dairy, churning butter.

"James!" Elspeth exclaimed as she dropped the wooden dash into the churn and hurled herself into his arms.

"It is good to see you."

He turned to the youngest, Margaret, who was always shy with him. She had only been seven when he had left home.

Was she reluctant because she saw through him? He would have expected Elspeth to be more resentful of his leaving.

"Does your old brother get a kiss?"

Margaret set down her dash and gently reached up and kissed his cheek. He pulled her into a hug and she squealed.

He picked up the churn and began to help. "This is harder than it looks."

"I would have thought you to have some strength after all that time in the army," Elspeth drawled.

"But I am an officer," he retorted in a haughty voice.

"Do you mean by that you are paid to give orders? That must earn you some respect," she answered dryly.

"Indeed. How long does this take?"

She lifted a shoulder. "As long as it takes. How long are you home for?" she asked.

"As long as it takes," he replied with her own answer.

She humphed. "You do not mean to stay, then."

"As a matter of fact, I do."

"Run along, Margo, and see if Cook needs help with anything," Elspeth ordered.

Margaret smiled shyly and scuttled out of the door.

"What is it you are not telling me?" Elspeth eyed him keenly.

He might as well confess all now. "I am telling you that we might have to sell the estate."

She plunged more vigorously with her dash.

"Mama says you have a suitor. I think you should consider him."

"He cannot afford to have a wife," she snapped and beat the cream as it turned thicker and thicker.

"But you would accept him if he could?"

She stopped and looked up at him. "Don't be daft, brother."

Well, that answered that. He would send off some letters that very day.

ANNAG WAITED until James went beneath the water, then ran to find Morag and return to the house. She was behaving like a silly little girl, but her feelings were too raw. It had always been a possibility that he would come home, but she had thought he was still with the army. Was he not a soldier by choice? Perhaps his father had died or perhaps he was just visiting. Why was she so flustered? It had been ten years, for goodness' sake!

He could be married himself, although would she not have heard of such a thing? Perhaps not, but her sisters were well acquainted with his sisters.

Deep in thought, she did not remount Morag but walked more slowly the miles back to the house.

Her mother and sisters were in the drawing room. Mama was

working at her needlepoint while Innis was practising the pianoforte. Fenella was looking through fashion plates.

"Where have you been?" her mother asked when Annag walked through the door.

"I went out for a long ride," she replied, pulling off her gloves and bonnet.

"What happened to your ribbons?" Fenella asked.

Bother. She had forgotten to conceal that. "They met an unfortunate end." She set the bonnet aside and did not elaborate.

Fenella was already back to the latest fashions. "Do you think this would look smart on me in a pale blue?"

"Is that a rhetorical question?" She had beautiful pale blue eyes and everything in blue looked good on her.

She waved her hand. "Yes, I know blue favours me, but what about the design?"

Annag humoured her by looking. "It has too many flounces."

Her sister huffed her disagreement.

"You did ask."

"I suppose I did," she muttered and flipped to the next page with dramatic effect.

"How is the Frome family?"

All three of them stilled abruptly and looked at her.

"What is it?"

"I did not think you would wish to speak of them," her mother said, needle hovering over her hoop.

"It has been ten years. I think it is perfectly normal to inquire after them. I rode near the lake and was curious. Do you no longer associate with them because of me?"

"Of course not," her mother said. "We have very few acquaintances of our station hereabouts as it is."

Frankly, Annag was surprised to hear her mother considered James' family to be of their station. That had certainly not been the case when she had wished to marry him.

"Are they well? The sisters must be grown by now."

"Elspeth is one and twenty and Margaret is now seventeen. They are not married, either." She placed a slight emphasis on either as though it were Annag's fault.

A look passed between her sisters.

"What are you not saying?"

"The estate is falling into ruin. Mr. Frome is in a decline and they have dismissed almost all their servants," Innis stated.

"Why have you said nothing of this to me?" their mother asked.

Innis gave her a look of bewilderment. Then they had stopped socializing with them. "Mrs. Frome had hopes of James taking over, but can no longer be sure if it is salvageable."

"Oh, dear. I am sorry to hear that. Does he refuse to help?" Annag asked.

"I do not think he knows," Innis answered. "Elspeth said their mother had never wanted to burden him."

"You must be glad to have had a lucky escape," Fenella said knowingly.

"That is hardly a fair remark, Fenella." she objected severely. "Things would have been different had we married. He would have stayed here and had my dowry."

"If your father had consented to that," her mother added. "There is no saying he has a better head for business than Mr. Frome. I suppose we should call on them and gauge for ourselves the true state of things. I would not be neglectful of our friends."

"What could you do for them? I hardly think they would take kindly to suggestions of charity."

"I cannot tell, but it seems worse to ignore the situation, do you not think?" Her mother paused again in evident thought.

"Could we offer to take the girls to London?" Innis asked. Elspeth was one of her dearest friends.

"If the circumstances are as straitened as you suggest, then they would only be more disheartened by having to refuse. Even if we house them, they would have no money for all the gowns they would require. You know how even your father grumbles about those."

"Besides, they are both prettier than you," Fenella added.

"That was an unkind thing to say. You had better improve your manners or no one will have you, regardless of your dowry," their mother scolded.

Annag did not know how much more of this she could stomach. Her heart was even more conflicted after hearing that James' family was in difficulties.

"I think it is too late to call today, but perhaps we may do so tomorrow."

Annag tried to mask her features from any reaction. Certainly, she could not mention she had seen James bathing in the lake!

"I will have Cook prepare a basket of preserves and honey. That should not be too insulting."

"No, Mama. We do have excellent preserves," Annag said absently, as if a pot of jam would make any difference. Her mind whirled with what all this meant. Would she be able to face him on the morrow as if nothing had ever happened?

"I wonder if Captain Frome is very handsome?" Fenella asked.

"He was ten years ago, although in rather a boyish way. I do not see why he would not be now," Innis answered.

"But is he scarred horribly, I wonder?"

That would be Fenella's first concern, Anna thought uncharitably. "Why does it matter? He is too lowly for you," she said quoting her father's words from all those years ago.

Her mother looked at her sharply. Her expression sent a clear warning.

"But he is a hero. It would be an advantage to be seen on his arm even if I would not marry him. Have you seen a man in full regimentals, Annag?" Fenella gave her a look, indicating she was a simpleton.

"Of course I have. I was married for nine years, if you recall."

"But you wanted to be married to him, did you not?"

"Fenella!" her mother scolded. "That is not something to be mentioned."

"Yet it is acceptable for her to behave as though using a gentleman for advantage is a subject to be spoken of?" Annag asked in disbelief.

"I do not see why we cannot discuss such matters amongst ourselves," Fenella protested.

"He is handsome," Innis remarked. "And not scarred."

"And how do you know this?" Fenella asked.

"I saw him not too long ago. He was home briefly after escorting one of his fellow officers' bodies home."

"Why did you say nothing of this?" their mother asked.

"I did not think we were to mention his name."

"I wonder if he will come back now that the war has ended or if he will remain in service?" Annag asked.

"You would think he might come to attend to his family's welfare," Lady McKiernan said primly.

Annag wanted to shout, 'He is here!' But she dared not, even though it would be satisfactory to see their faces.

"Why must we wait so long to leave for London?" Fenella asked in her single-minded way.

"Not until later in the spring. How many times have you asked me this and how many times have I answered?" Her mother shook her head.

"The Season has already begun. Why should we not go now?" her younger sister argued.

"The Season is only now beginning in earnest. You will be there in plenty of time," Annag explained.

"I have been waiting forever to go!"

"*You* have been waiting forever?" Innis swiftly corrected her sibling. "You are two years younger than I! In my opinion, I should be allowed to go first."

"You know your father hates London. You are both lucky he is willing to take you at all. If there were any eligible Scottish peers, you would be going to Edinburgh, not London."

"Do not remind me," Fenella snarled, yet again their mother did not see fit to correct her.

Annag wanted to tell them just exactly how lucky she had been to secure an English earl. She would have taken her poor Scottish farmer any day. *You still would*, her conscience remarked before she could stop it.

Just because he had loved her once, did not mean he still would.

21

Did he perhaps bear a grudge, even though it had not been her choice? For months, she had cried herself to sleep, wishing she had had a chance to speak with him again. Was there ever a worse fate than an unburdened conscience?

She supposed it was a blessing they were both here in Scotland at the same time and that she might see him and have a chance to speak with him, despite the fact that she could never change what had happened in the past. If she had learned nothing else in the last decade, it was that life was much too short to have regrets. It was time to move forward with life instead of looking backwards.

CHAPTER 3

*J*ames had buried himself amongst the piles of ledgers, bills and receipts—though there were not too many of the latter, to be sure.

He made a pile of what was owed, which was disastrous in and of itself, especially compared with the amount of rent coming in. Only three tenants remained and very little profit was being made from the crops. On the morrow he would ride out and see the condition of the cottages and farms, though he knew they would be no better than the manor house. How could they be?

His heart sank as he acknowledged their best prospect would be to sell up, but would anyone even want the estate in such a condition? Yet what else could he do? His father had not schooled him on being a farmer—if he even knew himself, which seemed increasingly unlikely as James acquainted himself with the true status of things. He hoped those men he had offered tenancies to would be willing to come and work the land. Who else could he turn to? He thought of his brethren, and the two most likely to be of assistance were Waverley and Thackeray. Both of them were landed peers and would have a great deal more land than he. Perhaps one of their stewards might be willing to give him advice.

It could not hurt to write to them, but first he ought to know what to tell them. He stood and stretched, cracking his neck in the process. He had been at the task for hours, he realized, as he walked out of the French doors and saw the sun cresting over the mountain.

"I might as well start now." The sooner he began, the sooner decisions and actions could be taken. Being idle was not his nature. Even when they had been encamped for the winter, James had always been out hunting or fishing rather than sitting about.

He went upstairs to wash and change for the day and passed Elspeth, coming from her bedchamber.

"What are you doing awake so early?"

She gave him an incredulous look. "Working, dear brother. It has been this way for years."

"We have no one left to milk the cows. Margaret looks after the hen house and collects the eggs."

"Who plants the fields?"

Elspeth looked heavenward. "Who has time for that?" She walked away, leaving him standing there.

"Apparently I do," he muttered, and wondered how he was to learn everything as quickly as he needed to in order to save his family.

He changed into his oldest clothing and made his way to the stables to attend to Sancho.

"Good morning, old friend," he greeted the gallant steed.

Sancho glared at him then promptly swung his hindquarters in his direction.

"I know, I know. You do not like cold and damp places, but you must get used to it, my friend. We are not going anywhere for a very long time, I am afraid."

He brushed him and saddled him, talking to him as they went. "We must go and view the farm today, but I will at least try to leave you in pastures rich with grass and clover. It is much more lush here than in Spain.

Sancho whiffled sharply, clearly meaning he would be the decider of that.

"You will grow old and fat here, my friend. No more long journeys across the Andalusians."

First, James went to see the fields, which were growing as many weeds as barley. He was surprised anything resembling a crop was growing at all. Had someone planted it or was this just old seed still sprouting from previous crops? He really hated the fact that he had no idea. He did know that the soil had to be turned every year and the crop should be rotated, but when was the last time any of that had occurred?

Certainly, it was not a job for one man.

James did not know where to begin. He certainly had need of an entire regiment, and now. Perhaps he would include that in his letter as well, that soldiers needing work would be more than welcome. Then he would only need to fathom how to pay them.

He reined in Sancho and paused atop the hill overlooking the farm where the tenant cottages sat a little way up the slope on the other side. That was probably the best place to start. They would know how bad things were and what was needed to be done.

The first was occupied by Farmer Campbell, the tenant he knew best and whom had always been able to prosper despite James' father's shortcomings. James slid down from Sancho and tied his reins to a rail.

He walked around to the field, because he did not think he had ever seen the man anywhere else. Campbell and his two sons were wielding scythes and stopped when they saw him.

"Master James?" the father inquired.

"Och, 'tis Captain Frome now, Father," one of the strapping lads corrected.

James held out his hand. "I will answer to either. How are you, sir?"

"We are well, considering," he answered cautiously in a thick brogue.

"I am glad to hear it, for I have come to ask for your help."

The man raised his hat and wiped his brow. "What can I do for ye?"

"My father is not well and I have come home with the intention of trying to save the estate. Otherwise, we will have to sell."

Those words made Farmer Campbell shift uneasily.

"What can I do?"

"I know very little about farming. I have offered two of the vacant cottages to some fellow soldiers and at the very least, the roofs will need repair. I also need to determine if any crop can be salvaged for sale."

The man looked at his two sons, then back at James.

"Wal now, we'll be a-finished with yon scything in a day or two. I daresay some of yourn can be harvested. We'll have some time to spare then to help."

"Are there any other men or lads hereabouts who would be willing to lend a hand, do you know?"

Campbell rubbed his chin. "I canna say. I'll have to be seeing who I can gather. Everyone is harvesting their own crops, sithee? Howsoever, my sister has some boys as might be willin' to give us a hand." He paused and this time rubbed his bulbous nose. "I hate to ask thee, sir, but can ye pay them?"

"Tell me what a fair wage is and I will find a way."

"My Jacob and Samuel can mend the cottage roofs for you and anything needed inside. They've had enough practice wi' our own."

"I am much obliged. I will assist as well, if you tell me what to do. I know how to mend fences and dig trenches."

"Most labour dinna require a lot skill once ye've been shown how. 'Tis simple enough."

"I like the sound of that," he quipped with a smile he did not feel. After what he had seen while sorting through his father's limited bookkeeping, nothing seemed remotely simple anymore.

"Thank you, Campbell. I shall speak with the other tenants now. Let me know what you need in the way of supplies and I will do my level best to see you get them."

He took his leave feeling a wee more hopeful. The little amount he had managed to save over the years, combined with the funds from his army Commission, would not last long but what else could he do?

It was likely he would have to sell in the end, but he would ensure the farmers were taken care of if it came to that.

The other two tenants were less helpful and more resentful. He could hardly blame them, but he did tell them the Campbell boys would be coming to repair their roofs. It was too little too late, he feared.

As he and Sancho walked back to the house, he stopped at one of the breaches in the wall dividing his land from that of Laird McKiernan. He wondered how long it had been thus, but despite the hard labour, he could at least see results quickly once such damage was repaired.

"Do we have any sheep left, I wonder, or have they all become one with McKiernan's?" he asked out loud, but Sancho did not respond. Sheep were beneath his notice.

James dismounted again and left Sancho to graze. He stripped off his coat and waistcoat, rolled up his sleeves, and began to replace stones one at a time. It was mindless, back-breaking work and he found the numbing pain a welcome reprieve.

ANNAG SELECTED one of her lavender half-mourning gowns, knowing it favoured her copper curls more than any representation of half-mourning. She had her maid dress her hair without any frivolous curls, for some reason not wanting to appear too young that day.

Her heart skipped and her mind raced with anticipation of the inevitable resumption of her acquaintance with James.

Later, when she had gone to break her fast, Fenella remarked on her sister's irritability. Annag could hardly explain why her nerves were on edge, could she?

It seemed forever until it was finally time to pay the dreaded call. She should have gone for a ride, but she was terrified of chancing upon James on her own again. What would have happened if he had turned around yesterday at the lake? Her cheeks burned with mortification at the remembrance.

To keep occupied, she had written a long epistle to her son, trying not to portray her sadness at his absence even though she knew to the day how long it would be until his first holiday. Having completed several closely written pages and sealed them, she had placed the letter on the side-table in the hall and was waiting in the parlour when her sisters and mother finally joined her for the outing.

What would he be like now? Her mind would not refrain from revisiting the same subject. Would he still be the kind, humorous boy he used to be? His body was now hardened as a soldier—she flushed again at the recollection—but would the old James still reside within him? She had heard stories, of course, of how war changed people—how could it not? But the James she loved... she did not think she could bear it if he had died. There was something sacred in those memories of him that she had held on to, which had helped her keep going, safe in the knowledge she had once been loved by someone.

Innis arrived first, looking very pretty in a white and green striped muslin with little embroidered daisies all over it. Her hair was the lightest shade of the three of them and was more blonde than copper. She looked like a fresh summer bouquet.

Fenella was wearing a pink frock with too many flounces. One would have thought it would have looked poor with red hair, but hers was a dark enough shade that it was surprisingly becoming. Annag did not think she would ever think of her youngest sister as fresh. She was much too conniving and deliberate for that, but despite her large nose and long neck, she was attractive enough.

Their mother entered the room with her bonnet and gloves already on. "Shall we be off, my dears? The carriage is waiting."

The three of them tied their bonnets in place and Annag left the house in trepidation. In one respect, she was excited to see James again, but she was more afraid to ruin her ideal of him and for him to hold ill will in her heart for her. Always assuming, of course, she told herself sharply, he held anything at all in his heart for her.

"This drive takes *hours*," Innis complained. "It is much shorter to go directly."

"But then we must walk or ride," her mother responded, neither of which she would do, of course.

"It is a very pretty drive," her mother pointed out after a slight pause, which it was. Slow, rolling peaks led to dramatic, sweeping valleys which were lush with the green foliage and bright wild flowers of spring. Five miles and an hour later, Annag was relieved to be released from the confines of a carriage with her family.

Fenella had begun on her favourite topic—herself—and Annag had tried to close her ears and watch the passing scenery out of the window. Much though she tried, she could not turn her thoughts from James.

Once they had arrived and alighted, they stood at the door for some time, waiting for it to be answered. When it finally was, a flustered-looking Elspeth opened the door.

"Good afternoon. I apologize for keeping you waiting." She bobbed a curtsy. "Lady McKiernan, do please come in."

Annag noticed her mother and sisters exchange glances of pity as they followed Elspeth inside, where she led them to the drawing room. The sights and scents brought back a flood of memories of a decade ago. It was hard not to notice the signs of decline as the carpets and curtains were threadbare and the smell was somewhat musty, not like the clean, honeyed beeswax of their own house.

"Please have a seat and I will inform my mother and sister that you are here."

Elspeth hurried away.

"How long has it been since you called, Mother?" Annag asked.

The Countess actually had the grace to appear disconcerted. "I have not been here since you left, as well you know why. It was hardly a comfortable association after what happened."

None of them knew, then, Annag mused, how desperate were the straits in which the Frome family found itself.

Mrs. Frome came into the room, looking more harried than Elspeth had, and bobbed a quick curtsy.

"My lady, I beg your pardon. It has been quite some while since we have received any callers."

"Forgive us for intruding," Lady McKiernan said. "Annag has come for a visit and wished to know how her friends did. I am ashamed to say I have made very few calls myself since she left."

That was more gracious than Annag had thought her mother would be, although she had, of course, placed the blame on Annag. Did time truly heal all wounds, as the saying went? Annag was not so certain. She felt a distinct bruise over the region of her heart every time she thought of James.

Annag tried to smile and answer questions about her recent bereavement and her son when they were asked.

A few minutes later, Margaret entered, bearing a tray with tea and some biscuits. She had grown into a beautiful young lady. She been no more than seven or eight years old, when last Annag had seen her—about the same age as her son.

A wave of sadness threatened her composure and having accepted a cup of tea, she took a sip to mask her melancholy. It was a mistake to be here, but she could hardly leave at this point without appearing rude. She would have to remain and bear the discomfort.

Eventually, the question she wanted answered was asked and without her having to show her hand.

"How fairs your son, Mrs. Frome? Will he return now, after the success of Waterloo, do you suppose, or will he remain with the army?"

Elspeth and Margaret exchanged a look. It had been subtle, but she had seen it nonetheless.

"He has but just reached home. He arrived yesterday, in fact," Mrs. Frome replied.

"Oh, indeed?" her mother replied as though she had received an interesting titbit of gossip.

"I am afraid it is not a moment too soon, either. Mr. Frome has not been himself for some time and has been unable to oversee the estate," she said nervously. On those words, she looked down at her hands.

"I wish you had dropped me a hint," her mother said softly. "We would have done what we might to help."

Annag was a little surprised by the softness from her parent, but perhaps she had painted both of them in too harsh a light because of their swift dismissal of James, ten long years ago. Now, as a parent herself, she could understand a little better, but they had forced her into a harsh, cold marriage. Would it not be better to be poor and happy than rich and miserable?

Her dowry could have gone a long way towards maintaining this estate.

Annag met her mother's gaze and was surprised by the tenderness there. Almost, she could believe her mother understood Annag's thoughts. Unhappily, it was too late in the day.

"I thank you for your concern, Lady McKiernan, but I cannot conceive how you could help. James is here now and I pray he will be able to turn our fortunes around."

"If either of your girls should care to come to London with us, I would be pleased to chaperone them," her mother offered even though earlier she had said it would be cruel to do so.

"That is indeed most kind of you, ma'am, but I am afraid we are not in a position to have them properly brought out. The truth of the matter is that we have no money to spare for the gowns, bonnets and accessories the girls would require. Further, I am afraid they have duties to perform here."

"I understand completely. Nonetheless, we do not leave for a month, should you change your mind."

Annag noticed Innis and Elspeth chatting furiously in the corner. They had to be plotting something, she conjectured, but what?

"If it is only a matter of gowns, I have a great number which your daughters could adapt to their own taste, should they feel disposed. I have no doubt they are sadly no longer the mode, but since I do not plan to go to London myself, I have little need of them," she put in quietly.

There was a resounding gasp and then silence.

"But you must go!" Fenella exclaimed.

Annag shook her head. "I am not yet comfortable with the notion of returning to London. Recollect I am just out of mourning." She turned to her hostess. "May I take a walk in your garden?" she asked. Mrs. Frome looked worried but gave a quick nod.

Annag knew she was being rude, but she could not bear the discussion any longer. *All this anticipation*, she thought furiously, and she still had not seen James.

As she looked around, she observed that the estate was in a sad way. Mr. Frome had always loved his gardens and his bees, but even those once tenderly nurtured lawns and shrubberies were overrun and wild. She found a bench and sat down, surrounded by overgrown roses, lilacs and rhododendrons. Looking to the sky in an effort to calm herself and not cry, she started when, without warning, she heard James' voice. He was the only one to call her thus.

"Anna?"

CHAPTER 4

*W*ere his eyes deceiving him? James wiped the sweat from his brow and looked again. No, the person before him in the garden was certainly Lady Annag McKiernan. Lady Calder, he should more properly think of her, he reminded himself.

She was seated on a bench in the garden, looking sad, and he watched her for several minutes without shame. For the last ten years he had been deprived of the sight of her in the name of snobbery, since he had never quite been able to forgive. Now he was home and being completely honest, he could admit the truth, if only to himself. Despite his wide experience of the world, he had met no one who compared to Anna and she had been the reason his life had taken the turn it had… the reason he had left home and fought for his country.

James could not completely regret what she had given him. He had become a man overnight with the first cannonball of the first battle and he had formed friendships he would give his soul for. However, she had also taken a great deal away from him, including his ability to love another… he had not even been able to try.

She leaned forward and plucked a bloom of honeysuckle from a wild growing vine, brought it to her nose and inhaled deeply. She lifted her face to the sun with her eyes closed and there he saw clearly the face of his beloved, for despite everything, she still held his heart. She was just as beautiful—if not more so—than she had been as a girl. Her cheeks were fuller, as was her body, but her skin was still as smooth as white porcelain, and her locks his favourite shade of red.

Anna.

When she wiped away a tear rolling down her cheek, he finally had the boldness to speak.

"Anna?"

She jumped to her feet. "James?"

He stepped forward from behind a golden yew where he had been loitering, and bowed. "At your service, my lady. What brings you to our humble estate?" he asked, then winced a little at his unintended sarcasm. It had become as natural as breathing to lace every moment of prose with the dry humour that had become his armour.

"I have come home for a visit and my mother wished to pay a call on yours."

"She is in the house?" he asked curiously, cocking his head to one side.

"You may think it strange that I am to be found in the garden instead of the drawing room." She looked down at her hands. "But when they began discussing plans to go to London for the Season, I fear I had need of some fresh air."

"You do not care for London?"

"I do not, particularly. I spent the greater part of my marriage in the country."

"I see." She had used the past tense, he perceived. Did that mean she was no longer married? For the first time, he noticed she wore a lavender frock. Could she, perhaps, be in half-mourning?

"I have just put off my blacks, and I longed to see my family. My son has just been sent to school and I needed a diversion."

"Ah." So many thoughts at once left James at a loss for words. "You have a son, then." *Gad, what a stupid remark.*

"Yes, just one. He is eight."

Not the parcel of brats he had imagined, James reflected, unsure what to make of that information. His sister must have known all about Annag's history, but no one had dared to speak of her again after he left. Why would they have? "I have no sons." He almost winced as the words left his mouth. He sounded the dolt his sister had labelled him.

"Do you have daughters, then?" she enquired with a small amount of hesitation.

He shook his head. "What I mean to say is, I have no children. I have no wife, either." Dash it, he sounded more mutton-headed with every word.

"I have no daughters either."

"I see."

"I am glad to see you safely returned. I read the papers for your name."

A warm flutter spread over James at that simple acknowledgement. "That was kind of you."

"Not at all." She looked directly at him for the first time, her deep blue gaze still as arresting as ever. "Are you to stay in Scotland now, or must you go back?"

"I am here to stay. I sold out just before I returned."

"Are you pleased with that decision?"

She would ask him the question which cut straight to the bone. "I cannot yet say. I was unaware of my father's condition or how desperate were the circumstances here. I must determine whether or not we may recover or whether the only option will be to sell, if that is even possible." He might as well be straightforward. Anyone who looked about them would see the signs.

"Sell?" The look of astonishment on her face would have been humorous to him at one time, but now, for some reason, it hurt.

"What a lucky escape you have had, have you not?"

"Please do not say such things. You are very much mistaken if that is what you believe."

What else was he to believe? Instead of clarifying, he changed the subject. "Will you be staying long?"

"I cannot yet say. It will be hard to go back, but it would also be hard to begin again here."

"I feel much the same, but I cannot leave even if I wish to."

They exchanged a look of commiseration and he felt a little more in charity with her. He supposed he should be angry, but somehow he could not find it within him. He felt emotion, right enough—but how would his anger benefit anything now? The only thing he seemed to have any true anger for was senseless loss of life. His friends had died.

"James?"

He turned to Anna. Anna, who he had dreamed about was here in the flesh and was a widow. "Forgive me."

"Where did you go? You looked as though you were worlds away."

"Perhaps I was. It is strange, walking back into the past, is it not?"

"Yes, such a notion is not quite comfortable. But you are not the same person you were, are you?"

She was certainly direct. He could appreciate that.

"No. How could I be? And, I suspect, neither are you."

"No," she whispered. She opened her mouth as if to speak again but immediately closed it.

A pity, he sneered inwardly. He thought it likely there was much more to be said, but there would be no opportunity now.

"There you are! I see the two of you have become reacquainted," Fenella said, smiling warmly at him.

"Lady Fenella, I presume?" James bowed over the hand she had flirtatiously thrust in front of his face. She was going to be quite the handful in London, he had little doubt.

"Indeed. I am surprised you recognized me."

"Deduction, my dear. Are you to leave for London soon?" She had finally grown into her nose and neck, he noted in a swift, assessing glance.

"We are to be presented to the Queen this Season," she agreed. "Will you be there? I would be very glad of a handsome soldier to dance with."

"You will not want for partners, my lady. Unfortunately, I must remain here."

"Oh, that is such a shame." She pursed her lower lip in a practised pout.

James already pitied the poor soul who would be shackled to her. Lady Fenella was the kind of girl who would speedily find herself in heaps of trouble. He would be mindful to stay clear. Although he knew he would never be allowed any McKiernan girl, no matter the circumstances, he still wanted no part of her.

"Shall I escort you ladies back to the house?"

"Oh, yes. Mama sent me to fetch you, Annag. She is ready to go home."

James watched Anna as she rose to go with her sister. She seemed as wary of the girl as he.

He offered an arm to both ladies.

"I cannot wait to go to London!" she exclaimed naïvely, as any young girl with a head full of dreams would. "But Annag says she will not go. Can you please convince her how grand it will be?"

"You are not going?" James looked down at the top of Annag's bonnet, which was shaking back and forth in the negative. "She cannot fathom that anyone would wish to be in London."

"I do not have any particular objections to London on occasion, but I can also comprehend why it might not appeal to everyone."

"That is because you are a man," Fenella said boldly. "You are allowed to come and go as you please. I must do what Mama and Papa decide is best for me."

"Fenella, that is enough," Annag scolded.

"Well, it is true. You, of all people, should support me in *that*, at least," the girl said peevishly.

Whatever did she mean by that? Intrigued, James wanted to hear more, but unfortunately they had entered the house and thence the drawing room, to find the remaining McKiernan ladies ready to leave.

"There you are! I was beginning to wonder if you had decided to walk home!" Annag's mother scolded sharply.

"I came across Captain Frome in the gardens. We were becoming reacquainted," she explained with a smile, although to James it still looked sad. He supposed she must still be grieving over her husband's death and her son having moved away.

"That must have been a pleasant surprise for you, my dear," the dragon said, swiftly changing her tune as James stepped over the threshold behind the sisters. "Captain Frome, why do you not come to dinner on the morrow and you may tell us all about your experiences on the Continent. In fact, you must all of you come to dinner."

"I could not possibly leave Mr. Frome," his own mother said, "but I am sure James will be glad to escort the girls."

James was thankful for his years of military discipline, or he might have strangled his mother in that very moment. Did everyone expect him to behave as though nothing had ever happened between Anna, her parents and himself?

His sisters and the two younger McKiernan girls were already smiling and talking again—more likely conspiring, he corrected swiftly with a vague sense of unease.

"Do you comprehend, now, my meaning about coming home again?" Anna said with a knowing smile.

"At least my sisters are pleased," he replied as he walked the four ladies to their carriage and handed them inside. Nonetheless, it was strange to go from feeling you had some control over your daily decisions to feeling as though you had absolutely none. "And people say the army is confining. Ha!"

The carriage rolled away, and with its departure, James experienced some very mixed feelings.

~

ANNAG WANTED TO BE ALONE, in a quiet place where she could sort out her horribly confused feelings. Instead, she was cooped up in this confounded contraption for another hour.

"He is very handsome!" Fenella said.

"But hardly eligible now, is he?" Innis asked. "Father would not let Annag marry him. Besides, I thought you had set your heart on at least an Earl?"

"I still have, but he is a war hero. It would not go amiss to be seen on his arm in Town," Fenella said primly.

Annag looked out of the window again, wondering if she could elude their remarks by pretending to nap. Sisterly consideration did not extend to how she might be feeling upon seeing him again, or the devastation she was actually feeling.

"I do believe he has rather more on his mind than how to make Lady Fenella McKiernan's Season successful," Innis drawled.

"I daresay that is so," her mother added seriously. "I am all astonishment still. I would not have believed their situation had I not seen it with mine own eyes."

"'Tis a pity. Do you think Mr. Frome is very ill?"

"I cannot imagine Mrs. Frome would have said so were it not true."

"May we please take the girls with us to London?" Innis pleaded.

"I offered, did I not? If their mother can be convinced, I am happy to do so. It is certainly the very least one should do."

Annag could not but wonder at all of this charity from her mother. Guilt was a powerful persuader.

"If Annag is willing to share her wardrobe, then the expense should not be great since we are going anyway," her mother reasoned.

"Of course I am willing. I should not have suggested it otherwise, Mama," Annag said in a tone of gentle reproof. "I have no need of last Season's clothing. Even though my gowns and bonnets were made before I entered my period of mourning, they should not be too dreadfully out of fashion, and I am sure they will be able to make such alterations as may be necessary."

"I do wish you would come with us. Can we not convince you?" her mother asked.

Annag shook her head. "I cannot. It is too soon. The peace and quiet to be found here will be welcome whilst I decide what is next for me." Let them think she still grieved for her husband, if they would but allow her some solitude.

"You are young enough yet and still very eligible. Would you not consider marrying again?" Her mother, it seemed, was not about to give up so easily. "This time you may marry as you wish."

"That is the least of my concerns, I assure you. I wish to be near Tommy as much as I can."

"Of course you do," her mother agreed with a swift pat on Annag's arm. "That is only natural."

Annag compressed her lips on an acid retort. "I would be happy to write to a few friends and request they add you to their guest lists. Once you are seen at an event or two, everyone else will then send you invitations. Polite Society loves nothing better than a crush."

"Oh, would you do that for us? Thank you, Annag, you are the best of sisters!" Fenella exclaimed, quickly forgiving Annag's defection.

As soon as they had returned to the house, Annag fled to the solace of her apartments.

That part of her life was over with. Ten years of wondering, imagining—of dreading meeting him again... how absurd that she was so affected by it, she reflected.

Why did she want to stay here? Was it wise to be so near to James? Where else would she go? Even though there were any number of houses she could live in, none had been a home to her. When Tommy's first holiday arrived, she would need to be settled somewhere, but she had a couple of months of leisure yet in which to make that decision. The freedom was still too new.

Being in her childhood home was not precisely what she had expected either, at this juncture, but soon she would have the house to herself and perhaps that would allow her the time she needed in order to heal.

After a few minutes of staring through the window, the confines of her apartments were not satisfying, so she changed into a riding habit and hoped some exercise would relieve her of some of the considerations bearing down on her. It was curious, that after years of suppressing her opinions and feelings—of being a shadow of herself—they all felt near to bursting from her at one and the same time.

Once mounted upon Morag's back, they cantered through the narrow glen near Kiernan Castle, then opened up into the wider grassland, then let the mare have her head.

The wind whipping in her face and the speed of the elegant animal helped Annag's nerves to unwind as they always did. When they were both winded, she found her favourite spot in the meadow near the large oak, and dismounted for a rest.

Naturally, her thoughts drifted to James, and now she was in a place where she might think about their interchange without fear of interruption.

Seeing his face up close had been more disturbing than seeing his body the day before. His eyes were harsher and more knowing, no longer carefree and smiling as she remembered. His face was lined from squinting against the sun, and a few scars added character to his fair complexion. Those hazel eyes had compelled her to speak freely— far more than she had ever done before.

Was she drawn to stay at Kiernan Castle because of him?

Certainly, there had still been attraction, at least on her own account, but she well knew that neither of them was the same. He was marked by war and she by an indifferent, cold marriage that had left a different type of scar.

Yet in their brief interchange, she had felt a connection, a kinship. Would they be able to be friends? It was wonderful to find him whole and hale again. She had prayed daily for his safe return.

Her thoughts led her along another path. How could Mother have invited him to dinner? Did she believe a meal and pretend civility could erase everything her parents had done? Subconsciously, she lifted her hand to her mouth as another thought trampled the others. However would her father take the news of their dinner guest—if he even came?

Was she being ridiculous to hope for some continued bond such as friendship? For there could be nothing more, she knew—ten years apart was practically a lifetime.

Yet somehow she felt the need for him to understand that what had happened had not been her choice. She had been made to suffer greatly for their youthful naivete, as had he.

Even though he had been polite today, there had still been traces of bitterness. She could hardly blame him. As she mused, she picked a stem of meadowsweet and meandered around the field, inhaling the dulcet aroma of the frothy cream flowers. Why was his forgiveness so important to her? While the answer eluded her, it was nevertheless so.

Lost in her reflections, she rambled over the green grass, absent-mindedly picking heather and bluebells until she considered she could bear being indoors again. Looking around her, she saw that without conscious thought she had wandered to the lake. Turning, she instantly began to hurry away when she realized where her steps had carried her. The last thing she desired was for James to think she was pursuing him.

She whistled for Morag to come to her since the horse was still on the other side of the valley where she had left her.

CHAPTER 5

When James returned to the house, his mother was waiting for him.

"May I speak with you?" she asked.

"Of course." He held out his hand to the drawing room they and their guests had just exited. His father would be ensconced in the study.

"I thought that went rather well, all things considered," she said, fidgeting.

"What were you expecting?" he asked.

"I do not know, but it is a relief for our circumstances to be known. I am tired of hiding it and pretending all is well."

Frankly, James would be surprised if there were anyone who did not know. It only took one look at the place, and not a close look at that. "I had not realized you had not associated with anyone the whole time I have been away."

"We see people at church and participate in the village fairs, but we have not entertained since you left, it is true."

"Was it because of me or because there was no money?"

She thought for a moment. "I suppose both, in part, but it is time to let bygones be bygones."

"By all means," he said sarcastically, but thankfully she seemed not to notice his bitterness.

"I am considering letting your sisters go to London. What good is pride to us now? I do not wish them to become old maids, working themselves to the bone here. It may be their last hope."

"You should have told me."

"It seemed unimportant beside what you were doing. It was not so terrible at first, but one thing led to another… Then Napoleon threatened again and I could hardly call you back, could I?"

"I would have tried to help, somehow, Mama."

"You were already sending what you could. At first, when I tried to help, your father would get angry. I would slip into the study at night and settle what bills I could. I let most of the servants go, which eased matters a little, but it meant your sisters had to help."

"You realize, do you not, that the estate will, in all likelihood, have to be sold?" He might as well address the looming subject, he knew.

She nodded her head while tears streamed down her cheeks. "If we can but see your sisters settled, then I think it would be a relief. If your father and I could then remove to a small cottage somewhere, I could care for him properly without having to deal with all that needs to be done in the house. I had hoped there would be something left for you to inherit, but I fear we have failed you."

James denied it. "No. You have not failed me." His insides were burning with guilt. He was the one who had failed. "I will do what I can, Mama. I am expecting some soldiers to arrive shortly to help, and I have arranged for Campbell and his sons to repair the roofs for a start. I am hoping to have enough men to bring in the harvest and then we will see where things stand."

"It is good to have you home, son."

He gave her a hug and she dissolved quietly in his arms. It was little enough that he could do for her, but it was something. He suspected she had not allowed herself to cry despite desperately needing to do so, for this was the second time in as many days.

Even soldiers had to cry sometimes. More than once he had woken up in tears during the night following a nightmare about Peter's or

Colin's death. Sometimes the subconscious knew what one needed better than the conscious did.

"Is there somewhere you would like to go? Perhaps south, where it is warm and Father can take the waters?"

"I do not know. I should dislike to be so far from home. But I could write to his sister."

"Yes, do that, and I will see it is sent off immediately. You would have to travel by the end of summer."

He left his mother to think on that, and decided manual labour was what he needed. His first order of business was to mend the fence between the two estates so the sheep—if there were any left—would stay on their land. Mending fences was something he was actually capable of, having added his mite when needed in the army. Of course, he could have ordered some of the men to do it, but as a lieutenant he had been too afraid to give orders, and had not liked to command others to do things he was not willing to do himself. Who would have thought at the time that such tasks would be so useful later on? Certainly, he had not expected to return to such poverty as he was now facing.

He found a hammer and nails, an axe and a saw and having loaded them into the cart in an old shed, set out for the western boundary alongside the lake.

First, he gathered some freshly fallen timber and hauled it in pieces to the largest opening in the fence. There were several places in need of repair, mostly the stone walls and hedges, but this was the longest stretch.

After removing his waistcoat and rolling up his sleeves, he began working. Unfortunately, his mind went immediately to Anna. At least, he reflected, the first meeting was now over with. Mostly, he was thankful it had been a surprise because, unlike in war, expectation would have been unwelcome.

He wondered how long she would stay.

When he had envisioned coming home, it had not included seeing her again, let alone meeting with the McKiernans socially. James was not a hateful person, but that did not mean he wished to subject himself to wilful torment.

Did they really expect him to come to dinner as though the past had never happened? Could they believe that if they all pretended that one little bit of history did not exist, they would continue in peaceful harmony? He laughed as he split a log wide-open with a satisfying crack.

No, he did not think he could be so civil.

Five more pieces of wood fell the way of the first, then he began to saw off the bark and form the logs into rails.

The drenching sweat and aching muscles were much preferable to wearing a false smile and pretending niceties.

In fact, he would rather return to the army life than be sociable with the clan McKiernan. He released another satisfying whack as he thought of such an undesirable thing.

Seeing Anna again, looking unhappy, was not satisfying as he had thought it would be. In fact, it only added salt to the wound he had thought long healed. It was best to avoid her all together, he told himself.

Shaping logs into fence posts and rails was not a simple as it looked, but after a few hours, he had mended the largest breach in the fence.

He was drenched in perspiration and not fit for company, which suited his mental state completely. It looked as though he would have plenty of time for reflection. How long would it take to set the estate to rights? Or at least put it into a suitable state to sell? The letters he had written to some of his brethren for advice had been posted, and he hoped some of the soldiers he had met with would arrive soon to help. In the meantime, all he could do was work hard and repair things one at a time and hope he could still find something left of James when all was said and done.

As she waited for the dinner party to begin, Annag found that she was nervous. After years of feeling dead to life, she was uncertain she wanted to have so much sensibility all at once. She was also quite surprised that James had agreed to attend her mother's dinner party.

Part of her wished he would not come, but if she were being honest, she wanted desperately to see him. She had thought about him entirely too much since he had gone away, partly from guilt for his having been banished to the army and her thus fearing his certain death, and partly because she had been unable to keep from spinning tales about what might have been. Never more so had her thoughts wandered to her first love than when she heard tales about her husband's *affaires*.

Time healed a lot of things, of course it did, but now that James was back, all the old feelings were more open than ever.

And now, she mused, he was different—colder, harsher and also mysterious—and more handsome than ever. Was he the same person? How did he feel about her now?

How would he react to her father? Annag had never quite forgiven that gentleman. They could exist in the same house without speaking more than bare civilities. Would it be the same case with James tonight?

She dressed with care, this time in a dove grey silk with simple lines and put her hair into an equally simple chignon. When considering her wardrobe, she had found little that had not been chosen for her period of mourning. Perhaps she would order a few gowns from the local seamstress while she was here. Mrs. Brown had been quite good with a needle. That also reminded her that she should have her gowns sent for. Perhaps if Elspeth and Margaret saw she was in earnest, they might take the offer more seriously. They were the innocent bystanders in this tale, no matter the history between James and herself. She should not feel guilty for what had happened between them, but she did. Had James had any notion what would happen to his family when he had gone away? Of course he had not. Neither of them had thought there would be consequences to their love, but there were.

When she arrived downstairs, the only person there was her father. She so did not wish to speak with him, but she was in his house.

"Father."

"Annag." He acknowledged her greeting and poured her a drink.

He handed her the glass of sherry. "Thank you," she responded. "Are you aware we have guests this evening?"

"Only that there are to be some for dinner. Is it someone I dislike?" He scowled and his large moustache went up at the edges.

"James, Elspeth, and Margaret Frome."

He grunted in response.

"We called on them yesterday."

"I did not know the lad was back. I had assumed he died at Waterloo like most of the others."

"No," she whispered almost prayerfully.

He eyed her suspiciously. "You are not thinking of taking up with him again are you?"

She opened her mouth to speak, but he forestalled her. "I daresay you can do so without my blessing, now that you are a widow."

She felt her cheeks burn with anger, but she did not wish to argue with him. "I have no intentions of anything at the moment, Father. Things are not well at Alchnanny. Mother has invited the girls to London with you and I do hope that, despite past differences, you can be civil. What happened was a long time ago."

"Let bygones be bygones?"

"I would like them to be. Our families were once good friends."

He grunted again.

Her mother and sisters entered in a whirl—Fenella wearing too many flounces and looking fancy enough to be going to a ball.

Her mother breathed a sigh of a relief. "They are not here yet, thank goodness. Fenella tore a flounce and we thought we were late!"

"Let that be a lesson to you, dear sister. You are not even dancing yet!" Innis smirked.

Fenella glared at her. Annag felt very old.

"I think I hear carriage wheels," Innis said, and went to the window. "Well, more of a cart actually," she corrected.

Annag supposed there was no longer a carriage or, at the very least, the horses to pull it. A cart was far more practical.

Again she began to feel nervous with anticipation, which surprised her after everything she had undergone. She had been married, borne a child, and had nothing to prove, yet when it came to James, still she felt too much.

They were shown into the drawing room and Annag tried not to stare. She had not before seen James in formal attire and it was a devastating sight. When he left Scotland, he had been thin for his height. She had seen his muscle and sinew at the lake, but now there was something about him in a waistcoat and coat that made him appear to radiate danger—a danger that was barely contained within his evening suit.

It had to be hard for him to be present. *Fool*, she thought, of course it was. She stepped forward to greet him with a smile. "I was not sure you would come."

"I could not disappoint my sisters. Besides, Napoleon is smaller than your father."

"I was wondering if you still had your sense of humour."

"Some things are not so easily disposed of." His eyes twinkled.

"It was one of the things I liked about you best. I am glad war did not beat it out of you."

"Captain Frome," her father said gruffly, announcing his approach. He held out his hand. "Welcome home."

"Thank you, sir," James replied, though she noticed he stiffened and stood straighter. Was it nerves or an accustomed military bearing?

Annag noticed he did not say he was happy to be there.

As they entered the dining room, Annag found that, of course, she was seated next to him. They were only a party of eight, after all, and her parents, as host and hostess, occupied either end of the table. Fenella, unsurprisingly, had made certain she was placed on the other side of James.

49

Being so near to him felt overpowering; it was too soon to face such a proximity with equanimity. Their legs were practically touching, and she could feel the heat radiating from his closeness. Did he feel as awkward as she?

"I quite hoped you would wear your regimentals," Fenella said wistfully to James.

"Alas, we only wear them for balls and formal events, but I am no longer a soldier so I am not required to wear them all the time."

"But you can still wear it?" she persisted. "There is nothing so handsome as a gentleman in regimentals."

"Fenella," Annag said in a scolding tone.

"Do not trouble yourself, ma'am. It is a common question, actually," he said—with great forbearance, she felt.

"What do you plan to do now that you have sold out?" her father asked.

"The time has come for me to take over the duties of the estate."

"So you are here to stay?"

"For the foreseeable future," James agreed.

Annag wondered if he would speak about the condition of the estate. It was a matter of pride, of course, and would only prove her father had been correct all those years ago.

"My father has been ill and the estate is in need of considerable repair. I pray I am equal to the task."

Her father looked up at that. Annag also prayed he did not say something cutting and ruin the entire meal. "Is there anything in particular you are in need of?"

"Besides funds, you mean?" James asked satirically. A grave smile shaped his expressive mouth. "Mostly, I need willing hands. I have arranged for some of my tenants to make a start on the most pressing repairs, and for some old soldiers to provide much-needed labour. I hope it will be enough. I left home before I had learned much about farming."

"I will be happy to lend you labourers as well. Send word to Anderson for what you need."

"Thank you, Laird McKiernan," James said with a hint of surprise.

"I fear I might indeed have to accept your kind offer—at least to get the harvest in."

Annag wondered what this change was in her father. Did he regret his actions of all those years before—or at least the harshness and consequences of them? Or was it that he no longer felt threatened by him?

"Will you be attending the village fair? Entries for the arrow shooting and caber throwing are rather thin, I understand," Fenella put in, with far too much suggestion in her voice. If she were not checked, Annag mused, she would soon lose all sense of propriety.

"I am not sure either of those are my particular talents," James answered with some amusement.

"I thought all Scotsman threw the caber?" Innis asked.

"I did not say I could not; the truth is I am not good at it... unless it is amusement you are seeking."

"It seems as if it might be a soldiery pastime. What *can* you do, then?" Fenella prodded.

"Ride horses and shoot guns?" he returned in a mocking question.

"That is something, I suppose," she agreed.

"Thank you," he replied dryly.

"We will be leaving for London before the fair, you forget, Fenella. How is Tommy doing at school, Annag? You had a letter from him today, did you not?" her mother asked.

"I did. He seems to be doing well, although an eight-year-old boy is not a very verbose correspondent."

"Most men are taciturn, compared to ladies," James agreed. "We stick to what is strictly necessary."

"We have little else to do," Innis pointed out, but Annag noticed the Frome girls look down. They had too much to do, Annag would bet.

"I have sent for my gowns, ladies. When they arrive, you may sort through them to your hearts' content."

Margaret looked up with a smile, but Elspeth did not. Did she not wish to go to London, or did she not wish for charity? Annag decided she would try to find out later, but at least dinner had not been the disaster she had expected.

CHAPTER 6

*J*ames could not have been more surprised by the previous night's dinner if he had tried. It had been a little awkward at first, but Laird McKiernan had been more pleasant— well, not quite pleasant perhaps but civil, at least—than James had expected.

James was not beyond accepting the laird's offer of help. Already up and breakfasted, with the sun barely risen, he was ready to inspect the progress on the tenant roofs and help however he could. He could only hope there would be people to live in them, and work the land again, soon.

By the time he had ridden along the valley to the first cottage, he was surprised to find the roof with a large hole in it.

"Morning, Campbell," he called to one of the boys.

"Good morning, Captain."

"What is going on here? Was the entire portion rotten?" he enquired. "Not that that would be a surprise," he muttered in an under voice.

"Aye, they both had rotten bits. We're going to patch them. 'Tis faster and cheaper."

"That is good news if there is a good to be found."

"A couple of men arrived about supper-time last night—some of your soldiers, I do reckon. Da put them in the barn until we can get the roofs finished."

"That was very good of him," James remarked.

"Neither of them should be on a roof," the younger Campbell brother said as he scrambled into view.

"How may I help?" James asked, ignoring the scepticism the young man obviously had about the injured soldiers. Dealing with the men returning injured from war was a common problem all over, it seemed.

He pointed to a row of long straw that was soaked and flattened on the ground. "That needs to be gathered and tied in yealms, or bundles. Once we have a few of them, we make a yoke of them with a leather strap then fasten it to the roof."

"Sounds simple enough."

"Aye. It's simple but not easy."

"Of that I have no doubt." James pulled on his work gloves, then looked up to see how large a yealm Campbell wanted. He seemed to read his mind and with his hands showed James the size of a circle.

"Just make the butt-ends even and tie them up tight. We will trim the ends later."

After making several yealms into a yoke, James happened to look up and saw one of the two soldiers hobbling up the hill. He had a wooden leg from the knee down. It looked terribly uncomfortable.

"Morning, Captain," he called. "Beg pardon for reporting late for duty. It were a long few days o' travelling."

James went to shake the man's hand. "No one ever said travelling to Scotland was easy. I hope it did not prove a difficult journey apart from being a lengthy one."

"No, sir, not at all."

"You have met the Campbell family, I gather?"

"Aye, sir. They have been very accommodating," the man answered. He spoke well, his voice revealing a faint twang of the county of Southampton; the son of a yeoman or burgher, perhaps, James mused.

"This is Seargent Gilray, wasn't it?" James asked.

"Aye, sir. Is this to be one of our cottages?"

"It is. It might not look like much at this moment, but I hope it will be more appealing when we have finished fixing up the place."

"Any roof that comes with a way to make an honest wage looks appealing to me just now, sir. What would you have me do?"

"Assist me in tying this straw into bundles, if you would."

The sergeant stepped in and helped, doing what he could. James knew better than to pity him or try to intervene when he struggled. He would do better if he learned to adapt without unwelcome interference.

Soon afterwards, the other soldier arrived. He had all his limbs, but half of his body had been badly burned, James had been told. "Good morning, Private Dunlap. Once the roof is mended, you will not have to sleep in a barn."

The man was shy, either from his normal demeanour or because of his injuries, for he gave only a nod, then climbed up to the roof. "I've had experience of thatching," he stated, and moving to the far side of the roof, began to fix the yokes to the face Campbell had already begun repairing.

They had been working for a couple of hours when another individual arrived before the cottage.

"You must be Captain Frome," said the man pleasantly. He was neatly dressed and well-spoken.

"You have the advantage of me, sir."

"Robert Bruce. I am the curate." He held out his hand. Accepting the firm clasp, James shook it, giving the newcomer an appraising glance.

"Any relation to Longshanks?"

"None."

"What a pity."

"Indeed. My parents have an acquired taste in humour."

Realizing this had to be Elspeth's beau, James tried not to be too obvious in his assessment. Without further ado, the slender clergyman was shedding his coat and waistcoat and rolling up his sleeves.

James was glad to see he had come with the intention of adding his mite to theirs.

"How may I be of service, gentlemen?" he asked.

By noon, the first roof was finished, their hands were blistered, they were covered in dirt, and they all held a hard-earned respect for one another.

As they sat in the shade in their shirt sleeves, drinking from jugs of ale one of the Campbell brothers had had the foresight to bring, Elspeth drove up in the cart. James strongly suspected the curate's presence was due to her thoughtfulness, but he had not asked.

Mr. Bruce jumped to his feet to hand Elspeth down. James watched their obvious, though guarded, affection for each other.

"I suspect you may have worked up an appetite this morning, gentlemen?" she asked. "'Tis but simple bread, cheese and ale, but there is plenty to go around."

"That'll do us very well, Miss Frome. We be much obliged to you," the elder Campbell said.

"The roof looks very fine," she remarked as she handed food to each of the men. "How does the inside look?"

"Dusty and barren," James answered. "It needs a mattress and linens at the very least." When they had finished their food, Elspeth packed up the hamper and the curate loaded it in the cart.

"Do you mean to do the other cottage this afternoon?" she asked as she took up the reins.

James looked at the Campbell brothers, who nodded their affirmation.

"Well, then, I will have mattresses brought up by the end of the day so that these fine gentlemen may move into their new homes."

"We are very much obliged to you, miss," Sergeant Gilray said.

"'Tis just a start, but it is all yours," James said to the sergeant while the others were gathering their tools together.

After a meal and a brief rest, they moved on to the second cottage. The work went a little faster because the men had developed a system of working together. There was a great deal of satisfaction in completing so much, and in knowing two hard-working soldiers now had a place to live. It would be down to them to make of the dwellings what they would. Hopefully, Gilray and Dunlap had forged enough of a friendship with the Campbell brothers that they could all work together.

"Now they are both habitable, I will leave it to the two of you to decide who takes which cottage," James told Gilray and Dunlap.

"We have already done so, sir," Gilray answered. "Dunlap prefers the more secluded one."

James was not surprised. "Very well," he answered mildly.

"It has been hard work but worth the effort. Thank you, Cap'n," Gilray said as they washed their hands in the stream that ran from the lake alongside all the cottages. It certainly was a beautiful place, even though remote and rustic.

"It is I who am grateful to you for trying. We can pat each other on the back next year if we make a real go of it."

Elspeth arrived then, driving the cart, and she was not alone. Another cart was behind her containing several men and Annag, of all people.

James stepped forward to help her down. He held out his hand. "Forgive my dirt," he said as he realized how he must appear.

"It would appear to be well-earned dirt. The roofs look beautiful now, even though that seems a strange way to describe them."

"It does, but I quite agree. It quite puffs up a man to hear his handiwork admired."

She laughed. "We have brought baskets of goods for the soldiers to put in their larders."

"That was very thoughtful," he said as the servants she had brought with her unloaded mattresses and hampers.

"That is the least we can do. It is good to see these cottages filled again and after all these gallant men have done for our country, it seems fitting we should do more for them."

"I quite agree. Unfortunately, once soldiers return home injured, most folk prefer to act as though they have not seen them while yet enjoying the freedoms their labours have secured."

"I cannot imagine what they have suffered—what they are still suffering," she said as she looked at Gilray with his missing limb and Dunlap, whose scars were mostly hidden by his hat, but not all.

Before too long, the two former soldiers were settled into their new quarters, with their larders full and freshly aired mattresses on old truckle beds from the unoccupied servants' attics. James suspected they would both sleep well that night—perhaps one of the best night's sleep either had enjoyed since the war.

"I will see that cheese and bread are provided for them," Annag said. "Cook is delighted to have more men to feed. She lost her brother to the war."

"Please do thank her on my behalf. That will be of great assistance to them when starting anew," James said. Filled with emotion from being here again, at seeing her again, he handed her back into the cart where her servants were waiting. Thankfully, he saw the Campbell brothers waiting respectfully to speak with him or he might have embarrassed himself.

"Will I see you at church tomorrow?" she asked.

"I expect you will," James said, watching Elspeth speaking quietly with her curate. Annag followed his eyes and smiled knowingly.

James walked over to the Campbell brothers. "I appreciate all you have done to help. More than you can know. Please tender me an account as soon as you may."

"As to that, sir, we have a request to make of you." The two brothers looked at each other and the younger gave the elder and nod of assurance. Clutching his hat in his grubby paws, the elder continued, "We was wondering, since the other two cottages are unoccupied, if as how we might beg the chance of them ourselves? We would work the land with your men and make it the more profitable by the doing. It would be more than enough payment in itself, Captain Frome, if ye would but consider giving us the chance."

James was speechless. Rapidly collecting his thoughts, he replied, "There is no call for such diffidence, men. I welcome the suggestion. Indeed, I should have thought of it myself. It is a capital idea and would answer the purpose admirably."

James had never seen the Campbell brothers smile before, but as he left them beaming, he felt better about the situation at Alchnanny for the first time in years.

～

ANNAG HAD ALMOST FORGOTTEN how different it was to attend church in a small village. For many who lived a good distance, it was their only connection with other people for the entire week. Therefore, it tended to be more than just a sermon, being also a link with humanity.

It was no small matter of consequence that Annag, not having been present at the small village chapel in years, was back at the same time as Captain Frome, who must be something akin to the prodigal son. Or, she reflected, perhaps he was not so considered? Sometimes people could be critical in such a situation; perhaps they thought he had tried to rise above his station. How curious was that, when there was no one else in the neighbourhood above their station. James had always been well loved, however, and she suspected her father was cast as the villain in that play—which he was, but he had also been trying to protect his daughter. That was a hard thing for her to admit to herself still.

She was unsurprised, then, that there was a great deal of talk when she arrived with the clan McKiernan. She could feel the stares and whispers as her family took their places in the pew that had been theirs for generations. In preparation for the ordeal, she had dressed conservatively in a modest gown of mourning grey, with a half-veil covering her face—to hide her own emotions as much as anything.

The Frome pew was directly across the aisle from theirs. When James entered with his mother and sisters, Annag knew exactly who had arrived and why the congregation was gasping, and she was proud she had enough control not to crane her head to look, like the others within her sight. Word must have spread of his presence, but very likely it was the first good view of him most of them had had.

The service would now be delayed because their beloved captain was there and he was stopping to shake the hands of every single person present as though they were all dear friends.

James had always had that ability to make everyone feel they were the most important person in the room. His nature was such a far cry from that of her husband, who had believed himself above everyone not of the nobility.

No doubt the coincidence of James' and her return at the same time would be a source of gossip. It was rather incredible even to her. For while no one might have mentioned in years what had happened between them, in small villages memories were long.

Innis and Fenella were whispering to themselves and Anna tried to hear what they were saying.

"She does not want to go to London. She still wants to wait for him," Innis was saying. Annag swallowed. Were they tattling about her now?

"Why would she rather marry a curate than go to London?" Fenella shook her head in disbelief. Annag released a breath. They were referring to Elspeth and her beau.

Aha, so Elspeth was serious about the curate. Annag had suspected as much yesterday when she had sought out her sister to ask for her help and had then seen the two together. Fenella would never understand how such a base thing as love could be more important than money and position.

It was too bad that the living her father held was passed down solely to members of the family. Unfortunately, her relations did not care to live in the country and relied on men like Mr. Bruce to tend their flocks.

Annag was not well versed in the Calder estate, and wondered if perhaps they had a living available. She decided she would write to Tommy's steward and inquire. If there was an occasion when she could facilitate a marriage based on regard and affection, she would grasp the opportunity firmly.

Mr. Bruce followed behind the Frome family, not seeming to mind the delay, since he stopped to greet everyone as well. Her father, however, did.

"The prodigal son has returned, so doubtless we will next kill the fatted calf and dance," he grumbled.

"Hardly the prodigal, Father. He returns a hero." She had just been considering the same thing.

He huffed out a breath. "I daresay."

"You seemed ready to relinquish past enmity the other night. Are you of a different mind this morning?"

"I do not think so. It has become habit, I expect."

As James reached their pew, he stopped and shook her father's hand. This elicited a few murmurs amongst those of the congregation who obviously remembered why James had left in the first instance. Some had blamed James, some her father. In all likelihood they were expecting some kind of fireworks show.

ONCE MR. BRUCE reached the pulpit, he cleared his throat and then addressed them. "May I begin by saying how wonderful it is to have Captain Frome home safe from the wars? And, Lady Calder, it is also a pleasure to welcome you home again."

She smiled and inclined her head.

It was difficult to concentrate on the service and the sermon, although she was glad enough to go through the motions and spend the time thinking about things other than her own situation.

Mr. Bruce decided to speak on forgiveness and the importance of looking forward in life, as though he had chosen that particular topic specifically for them. Was that not often how sermons felt?

"Today our lesson comes from the Book of Matthew, Chapter Six.

For if you forgive men their trespasses, your heavenly Father will also forgive you: But if ye forgive not men their trespasses, neither will your Father forgive your trespasses."

. . .

ANNAG COULD HAVE SWORN her father squirmed in his seat. She was glad the initial bridge had been mended by her father and James at dinner, but there was a long way to go to make the fortress solid again.

"...BUT this is not always so simple. Forgiveness is the responsibility of the wronged party, but reconciliation is the responsibility of the one who did the wronging. We read in Matthew, Chapter Five, that *'If I have sinned against you I need to seek reconciliation.'* Therefore, let us humble ourselves before God and make restitution where needful, that we may live according to His will in peace and harmony. Amen."

ANNAG WAS FEELING UNACCOUNTABLY shy as the service ended and they stood to leave. Her father and mother hurried down the nave, leaving her standing face to face with James.

She was not unaware of the curious eyes upon them.

"Lady Calder." He greeted her with a bow.

"Captain Frome," she returned, with a curtsy.

She was about to turn and walk on when he offered her his arm.

However she might have imagined the manner of her initial encounters with him, friendliness and chivalry would not have been qualities she would have expected.

"Am I to assume you to be practising forgiveness and reconciliation as instructed?" she asked boldly, addressing the still unnamed history between them as she placed her hand on his arm and they turned to walk from the church.

"Ah, but then we would have to decide who was wronged and who did the wronging, that we may decide whom does what, would we not?"

"In that case, I would say we were both wronged. However, I believe we have seen about as much an admission of wrongdoing as we may expect from my father."

He narrowed his gaze. "Was there an admission which I missed?"

"Precisely."

"But is it not still our duty to seek reconciliation?" He twisted his face as though perplexed by the notion.

"I cannot say."

"I will give it more consideration in due course. I bear neither you nor your father any ill will, so that begs the question, is there any forgiveness or reconciliation required?"

"How very obliging of you," she returned in a dry tone.

"Have I wronged you?" He stopped their progression and looked down at her.

She turned her eyes away under the scrutiny. "No, of course not." *You abandoned me,* she wished to say. This conversation was taking a direction she was not prepared to travel in at this moment. "I hope your new tenants are settling well in their new accommodations."

"I hope so as well. I will look in on them on my way home."

"Good day to you, Captain." She curtsied and walked away in haste, while at the same time trying to smile at everyone who watched, hoping her veil hid her thoughts.

CHAPTER 7

Why did it seem that as soon as one thing was repaired another broke? Laird McKiernan's man had returned fifty sheep, but a villager had come to tell James a few had already escaped through the new fence put up. In actual fact, as it had turned out, the woolly beasts had broken through part of a stone wall, so he had spent the last few hours working on that. Soon he would ask someone with more knowledge than he to come and make certain it was solid this time.

The sun was high and he had not yet broken his fast. By the time he had washed and sat down to eat, the post had arrived.

'Twas a mild irritation about living so far north, that the post did not come so often and then it was frequently bundled all together. How long had it been since he posted those letters? It must have been two weeks, he tried to calculate. Nevertheless, despite being surprised to see replies so soon, he was pleased. He would very much welcome some good news.

He opened Waverley's letter first. Of course, he would get right to the heart of the matter, James reflected ruefully.

Do you mean to repair the estate to sell or to make a go of it yourself?

"I wish I knew the answer to that."

Because if you only want to repair and sell, the advice I would give you would be very different. In order to sell, for example, you need not do more than fix what is broken, but if you want to remain there, then you need to grow your flocks and increase the yield of your crops. My steward has a nephew who he thinks is ready to take on his own position. Perhaps you can work out an arrangement? The Duchess has a fancy for a trip to Scotland, so perhaps we will see you soon.

"Oh, Heaven forfend," James said, smacking the paper down on the table and shaking his head. "That is all Alchnanny needs, a duke and duchess here!"

Even though the Duke could be a bit heavy-handed, James would enjoy having him there. He had been one of the first to sell out, after Peter's death and his own injury, but he still kept in close touch with everyone and had even been present at Waterloo.

Next, James picked up Thackeray's reply. He had a great deal of thought on drainage ditches and crop rotation, which, out of necessity, interested James for the first time ever. Matthias actually enjoyed reading about such things.

There was nothing from Philip, but his last letter had mentioned a trip to Greece. James would much rather be in the Greek Isles...

That only left Tobin, who was newer to farming than James. He had no advice to offer, except he knew of a few soldiers who were excellent with horses and might be interested in positions as grooms if James needed help in that direction (which, in Tobin's opinion, he did).

James laughed, as he knew Tobin would have wanted.

He finished his breakfast and walked around the house, trying to look through the eyes of a guest. His mother would be mortified to know the Duke and Duchess would be visiting, but James had not masked their situation, so they had a good idea of the quality of reception awaiting them. Waverley had slept on the hard ground as a soldier, just as had James, and he knew the Duchess had once disguised herself as a kitchen maid. They would survive. Besides, they were coming at their own volition.

James put on his hat and made his way out to the stables to check

Sancho. Dunlap was fond of animals and had offered to attend to him, but James did not dare neglect the horse.

Sancho was lazily chomping on some hay and oats when James found him. "I say, you are being well fed, at least," James remarked.

Sanchez snorted, but his tail was waving, giving away his pleasure at James' visit.

"Would you care for a ride or have you retired from the vocation?" he asked.

Sancho's ears perked up, which was answer enough.

"Excellent. I'll fetch your saddle." James knew he had already been brushed. The horse's golden coat gleamed. He was grateful Dunlap was taking an interest in Sancho. Gilray had a head for numbers and had been assisting with the books. Both had also been helping with the harvest and in whatever capacity Farmer Campbell needed. Bless the man for taking the two injured soldiers under his wing. If they all pulled together to work the land—including the home farm—it would make the place more profitable for everyone. Once the fields were tilled and turned, they could be planted for the next season.

James walked Sancho to the far edge of the estate, thinking to do a survey of the perimeter. Parts of the wall were still crumbling, but he had managed to repair the gaping holes.

They walked slowly, inspecting each area, James making mental notes of what needed to be done next.

When they reached the lake, James dismounted and led Sancho to drink.

"Good afternoon, Captain Frome," Anna said, causing James' head to whip around, almost without his knowledge. How had he not noticed her?

"Lady Calder." He made her a leg, which was ridiculous.

She smiled, as was the intent. "I apologize for trespassing, but I confess this is still my favourite spot."

"I am drawn to it as well."

Sancho looked up and made some kind of braying noise. "Might I remind you, dear Sancho, that you are not a mule?" James followed the horse's gaze to where he had spotted a beautiful mare.

"Oho, Sancho. That is looking a long way above your origins."

The mare tossed her head and her mane flowed.

"She is flirting," Anna observed.

"No good can come of it," he told Sancho firmly.

The horse clearly did not care and was already prancing over to where the mare stood in waiting.

"Please tell me there is no current danger of any little Sanchos being created?" he asked.

"I do not believe there is anything to worry about. Allow them to have their fun."

"As long as I do not have to watch," he quipped, drawing a laugh from her. "We shall turn our backs and gaze at the lake, shall we?"

"An excellent idea."

The horse made a great show of the matter, of course.

"Actually, I had hoped I might see you," Anna said.

James looked sideways at her.

"Have you, perhaps, noticed your sister's... shall we say, preference... for the curate?"

"Oh yes, Robert Bruce." He did so enjoy the name. "I have noticed. He would seem to be a good sort of a fellow. I thought to ask some of my army colleagues if they have any livings available."

"Well," she said, with a hint of guilt on her face, "I might have done already." She pulled a letter from the jacket pocket of her riding habit.

"What is this?" he asked as he took it.

She shooed him with her hand. "Read the letter and you will understand."

"Your son is offering Mr. Bruce a living at an estate in Cumbria?" He proclaimed the contents with disbelief.

She smiled, looking very pleased with herself.

"I do not know what to say. I am indebted to you."

She snatched the letter from his hand. "Nonsense. I am doing this for them. I would like her to have a choice."

She turned to look at the horses who were flirting with one another, presumably so she would not say what they were both thinking: a choice they did not have.

"It is very kind of you, nonetheless, Lady Calder. I think, if you please, you should be the one to tell them."

"Of course. I wanted first to make certain you did not object. Your mother did not wish your sisters to go to London because of their being needed to work at home. However, I have sensed she might be changing her mind. Elspeth still seems somewhat resistant and I believe it is because of the curate."

"I agree. It is my wish that Elspeth should marry as she chooses, and that Margaret should go to London if she so desires. In fact, I am hoping also to send my parents on a repairing lease."

"Matters are not improving? The village is rife with conversation about how much you have accomplished in so short a time."

He groaned. How could he answer that? He had been working non-stop, but the list of needed repairs only grew and grew. "There has certainly been a great deal done, but accomplished is another matter. I do believe Elspeth is in the dairy, if you wish to present her with the good news." He bowed. "Now to extricate Sancho from his amour."

She laughed. "That might be more difficult than you imagine."

ANNAG COULD NOT HELP but laugh at James' horse. He was so very fitting a match for his master's personality. He obeyed James when he commanded him to come, but he made his annoyance known by arching his neck and giving him a look of disdain before stamping his hoof.

The normally docile Morag was surprisingly reluctant, but she did eventually respond to the demand of the rein and stood still to be mounted when commanded. James locked his hands to help Annag to mount, and as she stepped on them, he thrust her up into the saddle.

"Thank you. Will you join me? I think it would be a good thing for her to know you have her support."

"I daresay I can spare a moment for my sister," he teased. He mounted Sancho, who seemed pleased his rendezvous was not at an end. The two horses cantered side by side—a little too close, mayhap —but cooperated nonetheless. Having reached the house, James unsaddled them and turned them out together in a leafy paddock beside the stables.

Elspeth and Margaret were in the dairy, cleaning the surfaces after the morning's work.

"James! Have you come to churn the butter? You always appear when I have just finished," she teased. "Oh, my word, Lady Calder, forgive me. I did not see you there." The girls curtsied.

"Good day," she replied, inclining her head. "Do you have a few minutes to spare, Elspeth? There is something I should like to show you."

"Yes, of course." She cast a perplexed look at James and then nodded her head for Margaret to continue with her tasks.

"It is a pleasant day, why do we not take a turn in the garden?" James suggested.

"Now you have me worried, brother."

"Is that not what brothers are for?" he returned with a half-smile and a twinkle in his eye that made Annag's heart leap. She remembered when that sparkle used to be directed at her and she had no defence against it. She must guard herself. They were now ten years older and had lived completely separate lives. He had shown her no more than friendliness, so she should stop allowing her heart to hope for other things. So much burden did she carry, perhaps he wanted no part of it. Perhaps he did not think of marrying. Did she herself even wish to be married again?

She followed along behind the brother and sister as they walked to the garden. It had been trimmed and tamed a little since she had first seen it a couple of weeks ago.

James led Elspeth to a bench and helped her to be seated, then Annag joined her. A looked passed from Elspeth to James. "What is this about?" she asked.

"I will allow Lady Calder to explain. It is her doing."

"I did very little, in fact," Annag said. She handed Elspeth the letter.

With a confused look on her face, Elspeth took the paper, opened it and read the contents. Her hands began to shake and then tears rolled down her cheeks. Even though her head was bowed, Annag could see them.

"Elspeth?" James asked, concerned.

"What does this mean?"

"That means Mr. Bruce has a living if he wants it. He would be able to provide for you if you should wish to marry."

Instead of looking happy, Elspeth burst into tears. Annag took her into her arms, but cast her gaze up at James, who looked to be feeling equally confused. He sat on the other side of his sister and took her hand.

"Please say these are tears of happiness, or else I do not understand. I thought you would be pleased, if not ecstatic."

Elspeth inhaled raggedly then wiped at her eyes. "Oh, James, I would love nothing more than to marry Robert, but I cannot leave Mama to manage on her own. If only the living were here! Now I sound horridly ungrateful. Forgive me, Lady Calder."

"There is nothing to forgive. I wish there was a living here to offer," she answered.

"I am here, now. Mother wants you and Margaret to marry and be happy." James tried to reassure the girl.

"I know she wishes us to, but reality takes no account of dreams and wishes. You should know better than any of us."

Ignoring this last, he said, "Go and show this letter to Mr. Bruce and determine if you may have a future together. As to the rest, we will resolve matters somehow."

"Is his receiving this position conditional on his marrying me?" Elspeth asked. They both looked at Annag for the answer.

"No, I do not suppose so," she answered as she considered it. "He seems a good man and deserving of his own parish."

"That is a great relief to me, thank you, Lady Calder. I do not wish for him to offer for me unless he truly wishes to marry me."

"I think you will find that he does, my dear. Do you know where to find him?"

Elspeth nodded and squeezed Annag's arm in thanks before she dashed on her way.

James remained on the bench next to Annag as they watched Elspeth follow the path back to the house, shedding her apron as she went.

"I am indebted to you, Lady Calder."

"I did not do this for you," she whispered. "May we not be Anna and James again?"

"If that is your wish. How long do you mean to stay?"

"I am uncertain. Probably until Tommy's first holiday. I am not yet ready to return to England."

He stood somewhat abruptly. "I must continue working. I believe Sancho has had enough time with his latest flirt."

She made to stand and he offered his hand. It engulfed hers and was strong as he assisted her to her feet. She tried not to think of what it felt like to touch him again.

"Has Sancho had many flirts?"

"Not as many as he would like to pretend," James said dryly. "But I will allow him his delusions because he kept me alive and has been a most faithful companion over the years."

"Then I approve of him as a suitor." She hoped she had managed to keep an earnest look on her face.

"Very gracious of you, my lady. Sancho will be pleased."

They walked in silence to the paddock where they had left the two horses. James whistled and was promptly ignored.

"No oats for you tonight!" he shouted.

Annag could not keep from laughing so hard that her sides hurt.

"I am afraid we must arrange another meeting for them or Sancho will be escaping," he said in a thoughtful tone.

"Has he done this before?"

"Oh, yes. For while he is loyal and hard-working, he is a rascal who rather has a mind of his own."

"It sounds as if he thinks he is human."

"But of course." James looked down at her in all seriousness.

She laughed again. She did not think she had laughed so much in ten years, if at all.

Morag came to the fence, and James saddled her while Annag put on the bridle before mounting. The more James touched her, the more her heart seemed to soften towards him. It was also nice to feel she had a friend again. He led the mare through the gate, then shut it behind them.

Braying his displeasure, Sancho ran along beside the fence as Annag cantered away towards home. She laughed again. What an odd horse he was, to be sure, but his personality fit James well. What fun they must have had together—or, if not precisely fun, she supposed one might call it camaraderie.

Would that she had had something or someone to feel affection for when she had been in the depths of despair. She had her son, of course, but now he was growing up and it was unfair to ask a child to shoulder the burden of his mother's loneliness.

Annag began to cry as though she were grieving again.

"Why am I crying now?" she demanded of the barren hills. She did not feel the loss of her husband, and she did not quite think it was because her son was away at school.

It could not be that she was still grieving the loss of James, could it? "That is a silly notion," she told herself, but then doubted the words.

Perhaps being home again and seeing him had reopened wounds that had been closed but had not healed, if such a thing were possible.

Once she reached home, and had handed Morag to a groom, she walked up to the house, where she could hear her mother and sisters conversing in the morning room as she removed her hat and gloves. Selfishly, she could not wait for them to leave for London so she could have some peace. What an uncharitable thought that was, she chastised herself, but realized she desperately needed time to heal. It was hard to do that under the scrutiny of her mother and sisters. It was hard to explain, even to herself, how she could still need time. But she did.

"Annag!" Fenella said when she heard her sister in the hall. She jumped up, clapping her hands as Annag entered the room.

"What is it?" she asked. Oh, to be such a child again. Had she ever been thus? Perhaps she had. That reflection drew a sigh from her. She felt so very old beside her sister's exuberance.

"Father has agreed to host a ball!"

"Before you leave for London?"

Fenella's head bobbed up and down. "Is it not grand?"

"Indeed." Grand was not at all the word Annag would have chosen.

CHAPTER 8

Waverley and his Duchess were set to arrive, and now Lady McKiernan proposed a ball? Of all the things James had little time or inclination for, it was a ball, yet the invitation was in his hand, and he could hardly refuse, could he?

Elspeth was set to marry Mr. Bruce in three days' time. Between the wedding, although it would be small, and preparing the house for visitors, it felt as if the house had been turned upside down. James' and Elspeth's rooms had been made as ready as could be for the noble couple. Hopefully there would be enough room for the child, his nurse and the baby that would be included in this ducal household.

James' mother was less than amused that they were to host such lofty personages. He smiled. He was not worried. They did not stand on their dignity, and they were coming to help.

Waverley had sent a manservant, a chef, a groom and some sort of maid ahead of the main party to make preparations and to give warning of the impending arrival.

James was home to greet the carriages when they rolled up the drive. As he watched the progress of the cavalcade, he was further pleased by some of the progress he had made in the past few weeks. The garden was nearly tidy again. The carpets and draperies had been cleaned and every inch of wood polished to a shine. His mother had been relieved when he had hired some girls from the village for help during the visit. With Elspeth and Margaret leaving, they needed replacement pairs of hands to sustain the status quo. He was hoping they would be above it soon.

"Welcome to Scotland," he said as a footman opened the door to the first crested coach pulled by matching greys. With a broad smile, Waverley stepped down from the elegant vehicle. He shook James' hand before inhaling deeply of the fresh air and stretching widely in evident relief.

He then turned and leaned into the carriage, bringing out a sleeping child whom he placed directly into James' arms. "Greetings, little one," he whispered as he tucked her close against his chest.

The Duke had turned to hand down his Duchess, who smiled knowingly at the sight of James holding the child. "She has missed her Uncle James."

"And he has missed her. Welcome, your Grace. I hope Scotland is everything you imagined." He made a little bit of a bow, which she waved away and offered her cheek which he promptly kissed.

"Your task for the moment is far more important than making a bow to me."

James liked children, so he did not know why everyone made such a fuss if he held one. His butler was hovering to organize the bestowal of luggage and servants, so James turned, with Lady Frances still in his arms, and led the ducal couple inside. "We have made many improvements since I wrote to you," James remarked with a grin.

"Do not worry about a thing. We are happy to be here and do not need to be fussed over," responded her Grace.

"I told my mother as much, but she would not be assured. Here she is now." He opened the door to the drawing room. At their entry, his mother and sisters rose to their feet and made curtsies worthy of the King. James could not hide his amusement. "May I present their Graces, the Duke and Duchess of Waverley. Mrs. Frome, Miss Frome and Miss Margaret Frome," James said in his best major-domo voice.

"My dear mama, and sisters Elspeth and Margaret," he added in more normal tones.

Waverley looked at him with the long-suffering glare he had used many times when James was under his command, but greeted his mother and sisters as though they were queens themselves. "Thank you for allowing us to intrude, but we do consider James to be a part of our family and hope you will soon return the sentiment."

"We should be honoured, your Grace. Please make yourselves at home. I expect, after your journey, you would care to be shown at once to your apartments?" his mother offered.

"Yes, thank you, that would be most welcome," the Duchess replied. She looked at James. "Shall I take Frances now? You and Waverley may then talk." The child's nurse was hovering not far behind.

"She is resting perfectly in my arms," he responded. "Go and make yourself comfortable. I know where to find you if her father or I cannot manage her." He winked at the Duchess.

"Very well." She turned to follow his mother up the stairs and James tilted his head for Luke to follow him. Having cleaned the study, they had tried to settle their father in his sitting room instead, but old habits meant that he often still wandered down to the study. Peeping round the door, James found the room was empty, so he led Luke inside, poured them both a dram of whisky, then sat in one of the armchairs.

"Things look better than you described," Luke said as he raised his glass to James.

James raised his in acknowledgement. "Aye, but I have barely scratched beneath the surface."

"It is a start. I have brought the would-be steward for your consideration. He will go through the ledgers and, if you should so wish, set out an order of importance with respect to the various aspects of the estate."

"Oh, I do wish," James declared with gratitude. "I can but hope we may make enough profit to cover the expenses and begin paying off the debt."

"How are you managing thus far?"

"By using the proceeds from my Commission, but it will not last much longer."

"Will there be a harvest?"

"That remains to be seen. There are other, long overdue, matters which are happening at the moment. The elder of my sisters is to marry in three days' time."

"Ah, the curate who needed a living, I comprehend? I gather he has found one?"

"Indeed. A neighbour discovered one amongst her son's estates. You see, I do have a friend besides you," James teased.

"You make it sound like a piece of clothing from the wardrobe," Luke drawled.

"Are they not all of a piece to peers?"

"Of course. So you have one sister married off. Do you have plans for the younger?" he asked, changing the subject.

"A neighbouring family has offered to take her with them to London."

"For the Season?" Luke raised his eyebrows. He knew, as well as James, the cost.

"She has a duenna, a dwelling and a wardrobe, all courtesy of said neighbours. Why may she not?"

"I presume these are the same neighbours who happened to have a living for the curate?"

"They are relations."

"Has she a dowry?"

"She has the Frome looks," James explained.

Luke looked at him with exasperation.

"She has *all* the Frome looks."

"I will be mindful of her, as will Meg. Suitors may apply to me for her hand, if you wish."

"Scotland is a distance to travel, true enough, although it would show some mettle should a hopeful put himself to the trouble. At the least, I can rest assured no suitor will be desirous of her hand to make his fortune."

Luke inclined his head.

"Will you promise me you will assume the manner of a brigade major, if and when they apply to you? That will give me some small comfort. I believe you have no comprehension how forbidding you appear to subalterns."

Waverley gave a wry smile. "That will depend on the applicant's stamp. Your sisters will both soon be settled, then; that is good news. How do your parents go on?"

"I am making progress to that end as well. My mother desires a small cottage somewhere warm, perhaps where Father could take the waters."

"That is something I could help with."

"Wait! Do not tell me… you just happen to have a cosy cottage on the south coast that is lying empty."

Waverley's lips twitched. "No, but I do happen to have a house in Bath since my grandmother fancied Society there. Would that suffice? And before you start spewing nonsense, I am in a position to be of assistance to you and thus have offered. The house sits empty since her passing, unless someone wishes to use it. Why, therefore, should your parents not make a stay in Bath? To me you are as much, if not more, a member of my family than most of the far-flung cousins who grasp for an acquaintance."

"Very well, I thank you most sincerely. I am hardly in a position to refuse, am I? However, convincing my mother might be another thing entirely."

"I will deal with your mother."

James could not help but smile. Luke liked to believe he did not get his way because he was a duke. The brethren teased him mercilessly upon the subject.

"What?" he demanded when he noticed James smile.

"Nothing, your Grace."

Luke shook his head and emptied his glass. "I must away now to Meg and Frances. I presume I will see you at dinner?"

"Of course. I have something I need to do before then."

Luke clasped James' shoulder and gave it a squeeze. "I am glad you have matters in hand, but I am also glad you asked for help. Do you realize this is the first time you have ever asked me for anything?"

"Is that why you came with such alacrity?" James asked in wonderment.

"Partially, although Meg really did want to see Scotland. She has an astonishing desire to travel, even though I had warned her you avoided it at all costs."

James laughed. "Thank you. I am glad you are here."

Luke scooped a sleeping Frances into his arms and left, his boots thudding softly up the uncarpeted stairs, and James went to collect Sancho. Having saddled the stallion himself, he then rode out to Anna's favourite spot.

"I was hoping to find you here." He slid off Sancho and let him greet Anna's mare.

"I understand you have company," she said, looking up at him with a smile.

"Word travels fast. I had meant to tell you, but it kept slipping my mind. Do you think Lady McKiernan will object to having a duke and duchess at her ball?"

Anna plucked a wildflower from the grass beside her. "Which duke and duchess?"

"Is she particular?"

"No, but perhaps I am."

James suspected there was some underlying experience from her life with her husband that made her wary.

"Their Graces of Waverley," he answered.

"Waverley?" she questioned in surprise.

"We served together. Is aught amiss with him?"

"Not at all. The Duchess was always kind to me, and is not at all high in the instep."

"Waverley is, from time to time, but we remind him of his place when he forgets."

"He forgets he is a Duke?"

"No, he occasionally forgets he is one of us—one of the brethren, that is."

"Ah. They have come for a visit?"

"They have come to lend a hand," he clarified.

"How many of you are there?" she asked as she absentmindedly plucked a wildflower.

"Five, now. Two were killed in battle: Peter and Colin." He knew she was referring to the group of his brothers again.

"I am sorry. You need not scruple to speak of it to me if it helps."

He looked at her then, though he usually tried not to. Her beauty made it difficult to remember that he was not supposed to love her. Yet here he was, clinging to the friendship she offered, like a puppy waiting for scraps.

∾

"Captain Frome is friends with a Duke?" Fenella asked with sudden interest.

"A duke and duchess are to attend my ball?" Lady McKiernan looked up from her needlepoint.

They were taking the news much as Annag had expected. "He assures me they do not expect anything beyond the entertainments you had already planned, Mother. He says they are quite matter-of-fact and will not wish a fuss to be made."

"He must have known of this visit for some time. It is quite naughty of him to have kept it from me." Her mother could not decide if she was vexed or delighted by the news, it seemed. Annag was sure delight would win in the end.

"Perhaps he wanted to make sure they arrived in time, Mother. Consider what a frenzy it has you in already!"

"Have you met their Graces before, Annag?" Innis asked.

"I have, although it is unlikely they will remember."

"What are they like?" Fenella asked, already a dreamlike look upon her face.

"I saw them in London at various fashionable events and in the park, on occasion. The Duke is quite handsome and the Duchess is... so beautiful as to stun the senses. She looks like an angel sent from

79

Heaven, for she has almost white hair and very pale blue eyes. They are quite unmodish, too, as they are very much in love and not in the least bashful about it."

Fenella sighed. "I want to be a duchess."

"Then you shall be kept wanting. Did you not hear she looks like an angel?" Innis retorted in a sisterly fashion.

"That is quite enough, girls. We must now rearrange the order of seating at dinner, and of the courses," her mother said, already fretting.

"Simply move everyone down a place," Fenella said, rather practically.

"What about the menus? Annag, will you cast an eye over them for me, to see if they are suitable?"

"I am sure they will be unexceptional, Mother. The Duke and Duchess will not expect any special treatment. Besides, Cook will have ordered everything in advance."

"Please take a look, nevertheless. We can always remove something if you think it is too ordinary."

"They have come because they wish to experience Scotland, not London. All will be well, I assure you."

"Be that as it may, I have no desire to appear shabby."

"You are in no danger of that, Mama."

"I suppose it is something of a coup to have a Duke and Duchess present... and you are a countess."

"Yes, Mama." That, Annag mused sadly, was about all the significance she had held in London.

"Oh, Mama, only consider! We will be friends with a duke and duchess when we go to London!" Fenella declared excitedly.

"That will depend on your behaviour while they are here, although 'friends' might be coming it too strong. Pray do not give them a disgust of you!" Innis warned.

"Miss Margaret will be accompanying us to London. She will have a close acquaintance with them, mark my words. It would not surprise me if the Duke did not act on Captain Frome's behalf, if they are on such terms of intimacy that his Grace condescends to visit the Captain's small estate in Scotland."

"I collect you may be right, Mama," interposed Annag. "Captain Frome informed me he and the Duke were part of a group he called his brothers, who served together."

"Would it not be better if Margaret stayed with them in Town?" Fenella asked. "Then we could have reason to call there often!"

"Of course, if they were to offer, then she would be foolish not to take the opportunity afforded her. But think, girls!" her mother said with an imperative gesture of her hand. "It would be equally propitious for them to call on her in Portman Square. I expect she would be more comfortable staying where she has company of her age, though," she added thoughtfully after a slight pause.

"They may not remain in London for the whole Season. They have a small child, after all." Annag hated the plotting.

"It will be a useful connection to have, nevertheless," her mother said.

"Fenella, do endeavour not to scheme. It is quite transparent, and I assure you people will like you the better for not indulging in such stratagems," Annag advised gently.

Fenella scowled.

"Good manners and pretty smiles will get you much farther. You may trust my word on this," she went on. "If you will not take my advice about flounces, then at least take this."

Innis burst out laughing, which could not be other than helpful. "That is akin to asking her not to breathe, sister."

"By the by, I have directed my wardrobe to be sent to the London house," Annag interposed firmly before her younger siblings came to blows. "I will also send a letter of introduction to the modiste I favoured. I know Margaret does fine needlework, and since we are much of a size she may not need to make a great deal of alteration."

"Hopefully, her pretty face and her connections will be enough for some eligible gentleman to overlook her lack of dowry," Fenella added.

"There will be plenty of time to consider that after our ball." Her mother began to rise but stopped when Fenella kept talking.

"Do you think the Duke will dance?" she asked Annag.

"I expect he will dance a set or two, but I cannot say for sure."

"Captain Frome was always a jolly dancer when he was young," her mother remarked. "He does not seem as jolly now."

"He has been away at war for ten years, and he came home to a frightful state of affairs," Annag pointed out.

"He seems to be putting things in order well," her mother observed. "Do you think they will sell the estate and remove to a smaller property?"

"The possibility of such an outcome was mentioned when first we met, but he has not said so again. Perhaps he spoke in despair upon first realizing what he was up against. But the cottages are now occupied and I hear tell he is planning to work all the land together with his tenants after the end of harvest."

"With Elspeth to marry and Margaret hoping to find a match in London, life would seem to be improving for the Captain."

"Is he the reason you wish to remain behind, Annag?" Fenella asked bluntly.

She looked at her sister with all the exasperation she felt. "I am remaining behind because I am ill-equipped to deal with London and the fashionable world. Is that not enough?" Why was she so defensive?

Fenella lifted a shoulder, a petulant gesture which further irritated Annag even while she felt somewhat mollified. Of course Fenella would not understand. She could not understand. She was little more than a child despite her years.

"I merely wondered if perhaps, given your history, that you might wish to rekindle your attachment."

"Fenella, do stop badgering your sister," her mother scolded.

"I had intended to stay here before I knew of his return," Annag said in a mild tone, with difficulty controlling her temper. "We have enjoyed several conversations, but only as friends. The only love-affair happening hereabouts would seem to be his horse with my mare."

Innis sniggered.

Fenella would not let the subject go. "In that case, there should be plenty of opportunity, should you desire one," she remarked rudely.

"Girls, that is quite enough! Come along. We must check everything twice—this ball has to be perfect! Has Mrs. Brown sent over our gowns yet?" her mother asked as she hustled her younger daughters out of the room.

Annag sat down at the small wooden escritoire desk in the corner, relieved that they were gone. It was so very exhausting being back home, although in a different way from at Radford. There, she had not been able to be herself. Now, she had to decide who to be—who she was. Did she desire an *affair du coeur* with James?

Shaking her head at her thoughts, she pulled some paper from a drawer in order to write to Tommy.

Sometimes she struggled with what to tell an eight-year-old boy. Did he miss her as much as she missed him? She suspected he was enjoying the company of other boys, but perhaps at night, when lying on his bed, he might be sad if his eyes did not close immediately from his exertion of the day. She hoped that was the case, because she was sick at heart both for him and for what she longed to have. It was better being at Kiernan Castle among familiar surroundings, but it was no longer her home. Radford had never really been her home either, because her mother-in-law had never allowed her that luxury.

Annag decided to write what she thought would make Tommy smile. She told him about Sancho and Morag and her friend James. That way, she mused, if they ever happened to meet, her son would at least know good things about her former love. Annag knew she ought not to be thinking such thoughts, but supposed a meeting between them was a possibility. One thing was certain, Tommy would not wish to be hearing about balls and dukes and duchesses, so she told him of her brave friend, the soldier. Maybe James could give her a story or two to share for another letter.

CHAPTER 9

*J*ames found himself surprisingly tearful at his sister's nuptials. Their father was, thankfully, able to understand what was expected of him and was able to walk Elspeth down the aisle of the small chapel to where Mr. Bruce awaited her.

Laird McKiernan's brother came to officiate the wedding, since he held the living, for after all, a curate could not perform the ceremony at his own nuptials.

It was a fine wedding, and James was pleased to see his sister so happy. Following the small wedding breakfast, all of the family offered false assurances about the state of Alchnanny and then the happy pair were waved on their way to their new life in Cumbria.

His mother was tearful, his father blissfully ignorant, and Margaret was in raptures over her first ball. She had become bosom friends with the Duchess and little Frances while Luke and he had been rolling up their sleeves in hard labour.

The new steward was not only helpful and competent, he was also good-looking, and the females in the village were making sure they welcomed him properly.

James was left wondering at his good fortune. A future of penury and destitution was looking less likely. The estate was still years from being profitable, but at least now recovery was a possibility. The land was being worked, bills were being paid, his parents would soon be settled in Bath, at least for the foreseeable future, and both his sisters would surely have respectable marriages as they deserved.

As he dressed for the ball, he realized he would soon be left there alone. As an officer, he took action then moved on to the next task, the next skirmish. He had come home and made decisive decisions to fix the estate, but now found himself faced with an unsettling dilemma. What would he do next?

For ten years he had been a virtual nomad and now he was facing a solitary, chained existence.

The estate would sail smoothly along with Mr. Barrett at the helm, yet somehow James sensed that if he left at this juncture, he would feel as though he had failed.

However, he did not know what to do with himself. He could work the fields, he supposed, but knew he would soon grow restless, being there alone with little else to occupy his mind. Would it be better simply to sell the estate and find a place for himself with Waverley's interests? It was still early to make that decision, but perhaps it would be for the best. It was not as though his father would be disappointed in him now. James knew life was too short to waste on trying to fill another's expectations of him, yet what did *he* want? It was such a new sensation to have only himself to consider now he had left the army and the rest of his family was settled.

He tied his neckcloth and combed his beard before looking at himself in the glass. It was him, yet it seemed to be a stranger staring back at him.

He shook his head. It was not like him to spend so much time in self-reflection or being maudlin.

"Wellington would tell me I had too much time on my hands," he muttered, going down the stairs to escort Margaret to the ball. She was waiting for him.

"What is this?" he asked as she turned around and smiled at him. He swallowed hard. Without him noticing, his baby sister had grown up and was quite beautiful. She looked dashing in her borrowed dress,

ELIZABETH JOHNS

which was far finer than anything he could have purchased for her. Of a pale green that matched her eyes, it made her golden hair shine.

"You look as pretty as a picture," he said.

She made a deep curtsy and fluttered her fan. "Why, thank you, brother," she said in a haughty accent, then burst out laughing.

"Practising for London, are you? You will take Polite Society by storm. Perhaps I should go with you to fight off the dozens of suitors you will attract," he said, holding out his arm.

"Do not be silly. Besides, the Duke has graciously offered to act in your stead."

"You will do much better with His Grace's guardianship."

"I still wish you would come." She looked at him with pleading eyes. It was the only thing she had asked of him. He had given her so little that he did not want to disappoint her when she was just warming to him.

"Did I hear my name?" Waverley boomed as he escorted Meg down the stairs.

"No, but I was educating her on how to handle you," James quipped.

"Unlike you, she is the model of decorum," Waverley shot back. "I have no doubt we will get along famously."

"I cannot argue with that," James agreed. "Shall we go? You are the prize attraction, after all." James knew the ball would be a crush once word was out that a real duke and duchess would be there.

"We will only be part of the attraction, I am sure. You are a decorated war hero, *after all...* and a bachelor," Meg said with a wink.

"A cursed thing to be," he muttered.

They were soon seated in the carriage and on their way. Mr. Barrett travelled with them, but chose to ride on the box seat with the coachman.

For a few miles they marvelled at the view as they rounded the lake and waterfall.

"Who will you dance with first?" Margaret asked James as the coach drew towards the gates.

"I had thought to lead out my sister. Are you already spoken for?"

Her cheeks flushed pink. *Interesting*, he thought. "Who is it?"

"Mr. Barrett asked if I might stand up with him."

"Why the impudence of the man." James pretended mock offence. "Perhaps we should have made room for him between us."

"English stewards tend to think rather highly of themselves," Waverley agreed. "Forgive him; he was brought up with a certain standing, being the son of a duke's steward."

"I suppose I will look on mournfully from the spinsters' ranks," James remarked in an exaggeratedly melancholic tone.

"Nonsense," Margaret said, rapping him on the arm with her fan. "You must dance with one of the McKiernan ladies."

"If you think to fob Fenella off on to me, you are quite mistaken," he whispered loudly in her ear.

She laughed. "I thought nothing of the sort. She will be the toast of London."

"She will be ruined before the first week's end is what she will be if her mother does not watch her like a hawk," James corrected.

"I cannot like her staying there," Meg said. "Margaret, will you not stay with us and allow me to present you? When we go to the country you could then stay with them, if you did not wish to go with us, of course. I am afraid Fenella will do something outrageous and you will be caught in the mêlée."

"I should hate to refuse their kind offer," Margaret answered, clearly wavering. "What do you advise, brother?"

"I am inclined to agree with the Duchess, if she is in earnest about presenting you. Lady McKiernan will not take offence, I assure you, for the connection will only be to her benefit."

"I will make the request on your behalf, so you will not be put in a difficult position," Meg assured her.

"We will make certain they are invited to our opening ball, which will be held in your honour," Waverley added.

"In my honour?" Margaret blinked in surprise. "Such kindness—I could not possibly—indeed, it is not necessary, your Grace!"

James looked at the ceiling. "Here we go," he muttered. "Once his

Grace decides to do something, you had better just smile and nod, Margo."

"You have learned well, Captain." Catching James' eye, Waverley smirked.

Margaret, however, seemed distressed. "Oh, please, sir. I do not want such attention. I will be happy with attending a few parties and perhaps, if I am fortunate, making a simple match. People will expect more of me than I have."

"My dear, you are worth more than the whole of London Society put together," Meg said, reaching across to pat Margaret's hand.

James could feel his sister shaking beside him. She was most uncomfortable with the idea.

"We will not force anything upon you that you do not desire, but you must be formally introduced to the *ton* and be presented to the Queen," Meg said gently. "We do not have to do anything overly grand. I am being selfish by insisting you stay with me. You need feel no obligation."

"Oh, no, your Grace. I should feel far more comfortable with you."

"Meg," the Duchess corrected gently, smiling at Margaret's earnestness.

"Now that that is settled, let us circle back to the matter of whom James should dance with," Waverley suggested, still with the wicked gleam in his eye." I hear tell of a lovely widow you are well acquainted with."

James glared back. He was trying not to think of Anna. Who had told Waverley? James had deliberately refrained from mentioning it. Had he been foolish enough to say something years ago? He did not think so. He had tried in vain not to think of Anna as more than a friend, but even though she was a widow, she was far higher above his station now than she had been before. He had lofty friends, yes, but that was not the same as being one of them.

How long was she likely to stay at Kiernan Castle in any case? The thought of having her in his arms again was akin to tasting forbidden fruit. But how would he avoid it?

"There was once an... affection... between Lady Calder and myself when we were young and knew no better. That was a lifetime ago and we are different people now."

"It will not matter if you dance with her, then," Waverley said knowingly.

~

WOULD HE DANCE WITH HER? Standing in her bedchamber, considering her reflection in the cheval mirror, Annag imagined James would be unable to avoid doing so. It was how things were in the country. Even though they had been no more than friendly, a dance would set all the tongues to wagging.

She wanted very much to dance with him—but without him being compelled to ask.

She smoothed her hands down her petticoats, sighed, and again dressed in a silk gown of lavender half mourning, since it was really all she had to choose from. Then she sat down before the dressing table and her maid styled her hair in the latest fashion of high curls, with a few teased out to shape her face.

She had avoided, as far as was possible, the frenzy of the ball preparations. Everything had been ready for days, except for the food and flowers, but her mother was fretting nonetheless. Annag felt it was best to keep her distance.

Her maid clasped a simple string of pearls about Annag's neck and then slipped her matching earrings into place. It was time.

In the country, they did not hold big formal dinners before dances. Instead, there would be a large supper midway through the ball. She had forced herself to eat a small repast to try and calm her nervous stomach, but it had not improved matters. She felt more on display here than in London. There, she had been merely another countess who received knowing looks of pity because hers was a marriage of convenience, where her husband did openly prefer his *cher amie*. She was not the only one to suffer such indignities, but it had been insufferable and she was happy to remove to the country.

Her parents and sister were already downstairs and waiting for the guests to arrive.

"There you are!" her mother exclaimed, as though she were late.

"Everything looks perfect, Mother."

"You are quite certain?" Lady McKiernan asked doubtfully, even though she had hosted any number of balls. Never before had she received a duke and a duchess, though.

Annag smiled. "It is equal to any I have been to in London." There were some hostesses who held outrageously decorated, themed balls and masquerades, but Annag was not about to tell her mother of them now. Such extravagances would never do for the country.

Her mother heaved a sigh of relief then ushered her towards the entrance where they would receive the guests. Many of these arrived early, just as country folk often did. The ball would end before midnight as well because country hours were kept.

"How many people did Mother invite?" Annag whispered to Innis as the ballroom began to fill. It was a large, draughty banquet hall and looked positively medieval, with its large, wooden beams, stone floors and tapestries of old. In the winter, there were two giant fireplaces which did little to keep the lofty, open expanse warm. Nowadays they used it solely for these types of occasions.

At last, James and Margaret arrived with the Duke and Duchess of Waverley. A hush fell over the room, replaced a few seconds later by a dull murmur of whisperings.

James looked ravishing—if a man could be so described—in his formal attire. He greeted her father and then introduced the guests.

"Your Graces, may I present you to Laird and Lady McKiernan?" James made the formal introduction.

"It is an honour to bid you welcome, your Grace." Her father greeted them with a proper bow.

Waverley nodded pleasantly and moved on to her, bowing deeply over her extended hand.

"I believe you are already acquainted with the Duke and Duchess?" James asked her.

"It is lovely to see you again," Lady Calder," the Duchess said, as though they were close acquaintances. "I was sorry to hear of your loss. I believe you have a young son, do you not?"

"Yes, your Grace. Thank you. He has just recently gone to Eton."

"Oh, then you must keep yourself occupied," she said with understanding. "It was wise of you to visit your family at such a time."

The Duke and Duchess moved on into the ballroom, but James lingered a moment.

"You look very fetching, Lady Calder," he said smoothly. She knew he meant nothing by it, but she still had to fight a blush. She was a widow and a mother, for goodness' sake!

"I think it is time to begin the dancing, do you not agree, my lord?" her mother asked her father.

"If you say so, my lady. Will you honour me with a set tonight?" he asked her with a wink, to her evident surprise.

Her hand flew to her chest. "Why, I have not danced in years, Rory McKiernan."

"Since it is your ball, I think you may be permitted to come out of retirement for the occasion."

Annag looked on with a slight pang of envy. Even though her parents had meant well, they had taken away the very affection they held for each other away from her.

Her eyes were drawn to the Duke, who, leading his wife out to the floor, also looked like a man in love.

She looked away, not wishing them ill, and yet still not wanting to witness their affection.

A pair of boots appeared in her lowered vision, then a long finger tipped her chin upward. "Well, that is hardly the face of a lady wishful to dance, but I think we should dance nonetheless. Will you do me the honour, Anna?"

"For old times' sake?" she asked.

James offered his arm and led her to the floor. He seemed to be thinking about his answer. "Perhaps for new times' sake? I have become quite good at blanking out the past, and perhaps it is best to keep it that way."

"I wish I could," she said frankly.

The music began. He bowed, she curtsied. Annag rued her outspokenness. She should have better guarded her tongue. Now she had exposed her feelings to him. When they stepped towards each other and their gloved hands met, his searching gaze captured hers. Annag instantly felt as though he could see through her.

"Was he unkind to you?" James asked, deep concern etched in his face and in the furrow of his brow.

Thankfully, the figure decreed she take a turn with another partner and thus she had time to formulate her answer. When she and James met again, he was looking at her expectantly.

"I was treated exactly in the way Society expects an earl to treat his wife." *With indifferent politeness, disdain, and coldness.*

"Something tells me it is a good thing the man is no longer amongst the living."

His look was so intent, so harsh, it took Annag aback for a moment. This was what James had become. He was anything but cold. This was what his enemies saw.

"I did not wish for his death, but I am not displeased to be free," she admitted quietly.

Why had she revealed so much? Now she had to force a smile as she went down the set with her uncle, the vicar. At least he did not expect her to speak, but only nod at his perceived witticisms.

Perhaps she had said too much to James, but perhaps not. Did he think he was the only one who had suffered? Maybe he had not thought about her at all while he had been away, fighting for his country. She did not doubt his heart had been injured at the time, but if the newspaper reports were true, he had gone on to perform acts of valour and courage. Worthy things.

Some people were adept at separating their feelings. Had he not just said as much?

"What do you intend next, Anna? Your family and my sister leave for London. Do you plan to remain here alone?"

"Yes," she replied. "Pray do not give me away, but I am very much looking forward to the solitude. Does it make you think the less of me? I hold my family in the greatest affection, but I have never truly had the ordering of my life."

"I understand your meaning. I, too, will be alone. Everyone will be gone from Alchnanny."

"Did you ever feel lonely when you were with the army?" She had imagined him in a tent, alone with his thoughts of home—even, perhaps, of her. Silly girl.

"There were times, of course, especially in the beginning, but Waverley was my first commander and made certain I had little time to brood." He laughed. "You remember the brethren I spoke of? They helped me keep my head."

"I am glad to hear it. I am very glad you returned safely."

A shadow flitted across his face before he mastered it.

"What is it, James? Are you not glad you returned?" She could not bear to think of a world without him in it.

"I am, although not perhaps in the way you might think. I am glad to be alive, of course, even though the fact defies all logic."

"It was God's will, James," she insisted.

"Yes, there is little other explanation."

"What is it, then, that puts you in low spirits?" she asked when he fell silent.

His chest lifted with some suppressed emotion. "I find myself not knowing what to do now that everything appears to be in hand. It will be years before the estate is profitable, if ever, and yet I cannot say if I am meant to be a gentleman farmer."

"How else would you wish to occupy yourself?"

"That is the problem. I know only how to be a soldier."

"Perhaps you should allow yourself time to consider. Do not make any decisions in haste. It is what I mean to do."

Looking down at her, he smiled a little sadly. "You proffer wise counsel, Lady Calder."

He bowed to her and immediately she was conscious she did not want that to be the end.

CHAPTER 10

*D*ancing had been important to Wellington, and James supposed it could be enjoyable at times, but he always felt like a hanger-on and not anyone of import. Most of his fellow officers were either landed peers themselves or second sons of someone lofty, but not James. Perhaps he was refining too much upon it, but after being rejected by McKiernan for that reason, the notion had stuck.

Therefore, he had made it his mission to seek out those who needed a partner, those who might be less desirable themselves for whatever reason.

When the Duchess stopped him on his way to the line of hopefuls waiting for partners, he was somewhat surprised when she indicated she wanted to dance.

"May I not have a turn?" she asked, with a gleam in her eye. Waverley's charms must be fading, James thought wickedly.

"What the Duchess wishes for, the Duchess shall have, mayhap?" he responded roguishly. "It would be my pleasure, your Grace." He held out his arm to her.

"I do hope I am not keeping you from any lady in particular."

He looked over at the wallflowers and spinsters. "No indeed, ma'am. No one in particular."

"Fear not, Captain. I shall not trouble you after this dance. I have had little opportunity to speak with you, and since we leave tomorrow, this might be my last chance."

"Pray forgive my oversight in not requesting the honour of your company, your Grace," he teased. "I assumed there would be a line of partners vying to lead you out. You have my undivided attention, ma'am." He dipped his head in self-mockery.

She smiled. "It is not as serious as that."

"I must thank you for offering your patronage to my sister, for arranging escort of our parents to Bath, and also for coming all the way to Scotland with a steward in your train. I should, perhaps, rename Alchnanny 'Waverley Court' and have done," he added sardonically.

"It was our pleasure, and you know Luke really likes nothing more than to help people. Sometimes his title makes him feel as though he does not do enough."

"Luke feel inadequate? Will wonders never cease? He has practically saved my estate single-handedly but I will not be the one to tell him so."

She laughed. "He is inordinately fond and would do anything for each of you."

"Yes, I know. Had I not been in such desperate straits, I would not have asked."

"He also knows that."

The set began and although there was less time for serious speech, the Duchess still managed to get straight to the heart of the matter.

"I hope you will consider Lady Calder."

James would have missed a step had he not, at that moment, been standing still, awaiting his next part in the figure.

"Consider her for what?"

"Do try not to be dense, James. We know all about your history together: that you were betrothed but her father did not approve and sent you packing."

"That is so," he answered a little stiffly. "Why, then, should her father approve now?"

"She is a widow. She may make her own decisions."

He shook his head. "That is all in the past. I am glad we are now friends, which is more than I had ever thought to be when I left here a decade ago, but we are nothing more."

"I see how she looks at you, James."

What look could she mean? "I have nothing to offer her, Meg. You yourself have seen in what state of dilapidation is my estate."

Meg looked up at him with exasperation. He had seen his mother wear that same look many a time at his expense. "Perhaps so, yet it is an estate which has far more hope now than it did two months ago. Promise me you will consider it. Her marriage was not a happy one, I think."

"What do you mean?" Anna had hinted at difficulties, but had not given any specifics.

"It is not my place to say, of course, but Calder was rather notorious."

"In what way?"

Meg waited to answer until they came close together again. "He was notorious for preferring his mistress. He was always seen with her. Once his wife became with child, he took her to the country and left her there."

James stiffened with anger.

"It is not unusual, of course, for gentlemen to have mistresses, but they are usually discreet about it. It is not spoken of."

"You are saying Calder flaunted her before the *ton*?"

Meg nodded.

No wonder Anna had said what she had earlier, he thought furiously. "It does not mean she would now wish to be shackled to a poor farmer. She is more like to have a morbid distaste for matrimony."

"Maybe she will—and maybe she would care to wed a poor farmer. That would be her decision to make. I am merely asking you to consider it. Once all of us have left, you will both be here... unaccompanied except for servants..." she said, with a knowing smile which could almost be described as a smirk.

"I had not thought you to be a schemer, your Grace."

"I should love for you to know the happiness that Luke and I share." She laughed. "I *have* become a scheming matron, have I not?"

"Love and marriage is not in the stars for everyone." He had spent ten long years trying not to think of Anna, but had consoled himself with the belief that she was happy. Subconsciously, he looked around and found Anna dancing with the Duke. "Is he having this same conversation with her?"

"It would not surprise me, although I doubt she will take as much convincing as you."

"I think you both have attics to let. No offence intended, your Grace."

"None taken, Captain. Sometimes it is easier for others to see what is under one's nose."

"Are you inferring I cannot see the wood for the trees?"

"Precisely."

He did not want to allow himself to be hurt again. The loss of Anna had helped to shape who he was and he could not regret that, but it was much easier to keep a wall about his heart now. Being a soldier had made him adept at that.

His sister twirled by in the arms of Mr. Barrett, looking at him as though he were her favourite dessert. They had had two dances already.

"Oh, dear," he remarked. "I daresay it is a good thing she is leaving with you tomorrow."

"That is how Lady Calder looks at you."

"I beg to differ."

Meg looked up at the ceiling with a heavy sigh. He often compelled such reactions. "It would not be a terrible match," she said, "but I do believe that seeing what London has to offer will be best for Margaret at this juncture. If her heart still desires Mr. Barrett by the end of the Season, then you should consider it. He comes from a very good family and has the support of the Waverley duchy."

"I will, of course, take that into consideration. It is hard to think of her as being old enough to marry."

"She will be much sought after, despite her lack of fortune."

James made a face.

"Have no fear, Luke will manage her suitors well. It will be good practice for him."

"Poor Frances."

"Indeed." The dance ended and he escorted her back to Waverley. Anna was standing with him. Since that was the supper dance, why do we not all go in and sit together?" the Duke suggested as he pointedly took his wife's arm and practically forced James together with Anna.

"An excellent notion, as long as Lady Calder cares to join us," James said.

"Yes, of course." She took his arm and he allowed himself to consider what the Duchess had said. Was Anna truly open to his suit?

They walked to the other end of the banquet hall, where tables had been placed for supper. "I do hope there is some haggis," the Duchess said, shocking both James and Anna into a laugh.

"What is so amusing? I have wished to try it for some years. I thought it was a most proper Scottish food."

"It is certainly Scottish," James replied.

"Oh, how mortified would my mother be to know the Duchess wanted haggis. She would have me scrutinize the menus and remove anything which might be deemed common," Anna whispered to James. "Pardon me for a moment while I ask Cook if she might prepare some for her Grace."

"Of course. I will fill a plate for your return."

"Thank you. My tastes are very much the same," she said, giving his arm a light squeeze before she hurried away to find the cook.

He filled Anna's plate with lobster patties, scallops and tattie cakes. Much to his surprise, he had not forgotten. When he took the plates to the table, she had still not returned.

"Where is Lady Calder?" the Duchess enquired.

"She had something to attend to but said she would come back shortly. Please do not wait upon her return."

The Duke then appeared with her Grace's plate. "I did not see any haggis, my dear, but it is possible I missed it among the tremendous array of dishes."

Anna returned in a somewhat breathless whirl, holding a plate of the sausages. "I saw them replace the haggis when I was returning from the retiring room, so I took the liberty…"

The Duchess's face lit up with delight. "Oh, how thoughtful you are!"

"Let us hope she still smiles after she has taken her first bite," James said ruefully to Anna.

"This is delicious!" her Grace exclaimed, having swallowed her first mouthful, and Anna almost choked on her lobster patty.

~

AFTER SUPPER, many of the village folk began to leave, but there were a few who seemed determined to stay for the last couple of sets. Annag decided to escape outside for some fresh air.

The cool breeze was welcome as Annag sat down on a bench. Were it daylight, she would be able to see out over the valley to the lake below. The old castle sat high atop a cliff, surrounded by a stone wall and keep. It had been necessary, in times gone by, to defend it from the English.

Back in the present, Annag's feet hurt terribly from dancing a few sets. Her feet were out of practice. She had decided to take a moment to escape into the gardens and rest. Her mother might scold, but Annag was a widow now, as she had been reminded several times already during the course of the evening. A little laugh rolled out of her as she thought of the proposal she had received that night from Baron Cowan.

"As it happens, I am in need of a wife for my five children. What say you, my Lady Calder?"

"As honoured as I am by your offer, sir, I fear I must decline. I am not yet equal to such a task," she said, while trying not to laugh. She could not think of anything that would compel her to be tempted into marriage with the Baron. He was in all things the complete opposite of James.

"I must stop thinking that way," she told herself, looking up at the dusky sky scattered with stars.

"In what way must you stop thinking?"

She jumped. "It is not very gentlemanly to sneak up on a lady alone." Thank goodness she had not said his name aloud—had she?

"I was not sneaking. I would say you were wool-gathering and did not notice my approach. May I?" With his hand he indicated the seat next to her on the bench.

"Yes, of course." She edged over to make room. When he sat down, she felt engulfed by his presence.

"Are you enjoying yourself?" he asked.

"I have received a marriage proposal already this evening, if that is an indication of enjoyment," she said, attempting to speak with sincerity.

"Let me guess. Baron Cowan, perchance?

"However did you know?"

"I am sorry to disappoint you, but I believe he also made offers to my sister and both of yours."

"There is an end to the matter, then." She pretended disappointment. "And yourself, sir? Have you been made any offers which you may divulge?"

"Not offers, per se, but some very strong hints that my addresses would be welcome."

"Oh, I can imagine far too readily, and can only offer my apologies if one of them was from my sister."

"No, she made it quite clear I was of no interest unless I was in uniform."

"She does love a man in uniform," they said in unison and then laughed.

"One must hope there will not be too many uniforms in London to distract her from her purpose," James remarked.

Annag sighed. "I am not certain what her purpose is, James. I only pray she does not find herself in trouble."

"As you did?"

"That was uncalled for," she scolded. "It hardly gives credence to my parents' judgement that they thought you were a poor choice."

"I thank you," he said, sounding humbled.

"Nevertheless, Fenella finds a way to get what she wants without troubling her conscience. I believe my parents have become lax with her."

"It is often the way with the youngest, is it not?" James teased. "Although Margaret seems to be a sweet child."

"I am glad she will be with the Duchess. I am exhausted simply by being in a household with my mother and Fenella. If the party consisted only of Innis, I might consider going back to London for her."

"You really do not miss Town, then?"

"I am certain there are good parts to Society; sadly I did not happen to experience them."

"You knew none of its pleasures? The opera, the plays, the balls?"

"Unfortunately, my husband preferred to escort his mistress to such events rather than me."

"Forgive me, that was a horrid circumstance to have reminded you of."

"How could you have known? Most marriages maintain at least the pretence of being a couple. At the very least, I may give Calder credit for not going to the bother of fabricating such falsehoods."

"Are we not all false to some extent?"

"In what way do you mean?"

"Wellington liked to host balls. Often we would fight one day and dance the next."

"That is so..." She could not find the word.

"Strange? Ironic? It does bewilder the mind. Except, when you have seen the desperation of battle, it does help you carry on and forget what you have done."

"I conjecture you mean you then consider previous events as part of your duty and no more?" she asked, trying to make sense of it.

"Precisely. But it is not quite so easy as it sounds."

"I imagine not."

They spent some time in silent contemplation before James spoke again. "Did Waverley harass you?"

"About you, do you mean?" The Duke had spoken to her about James—not very subtly suggesting she consider him as a suitor. He must have been told there had once been some affection between them.

"Yes."

"He certainly sang your praises, but I did not take offence. He wants only what is best for you."

"Be that as it may, he is still a duke and expects to get what he wants."

"Did the Duchess press you in the same manner?" she asked, with much surprise.

"Rather more subtly than Waverley did, I would wager."

"Is it not ironic that people are trying to make a match between us?"

"Kindly take note they were not your parents," he said, not troubling to mask his evident bitterness.

"My parents no longer have the right to command me, James." Her boldness knew no bounds, it seemed.

He looked up at the stars, either contemplating her words or perhaps thinking of nothing at all.

She would not throw herself at him. She had said enough to indicate her interest. If he cared for her in the way she hoped, if he reciprocated her feelings... then he must address her in such terms.

"I am glad we can be friends, Anna," he said softly, still looking upward.

"Friends?" she echoed.

When there was a break in the music, it was quiet enough to hear the falls flowing down to the lake. With James next to her, strong and warm, it was the closest she had felt to peace in some time.

"Tell me about your son," he said suddenly, breaking the harmony.

"Tommy?" She felt herself smile. "He is of all things the most important to me."

"Does he resemble you?"

"I suppose he does, although he has bright blue eyes and adorable dimples when he smiles."

"He will be a charmer, then," James predicted.

"Perhaps so, if he has time for the ladies. At the moment his head is full of nothing but horses and cricket."

"School will be easier for him if he is an athlete."

"I daresay you are in the right of it. He does like to read, but not as much as he likes to ride."

"He sounds like most gentlemen of my acquaintance. Maybe one day I will be fortunate enough to meet him."

"I would like that," she said, her throat filling with tears. "I was not prepared for him to go, James. He is only eight. He should still be with his mother."

"When he had just lost his father, too."

"I am not sure that quite registered with him. He might have seen my husband once a year." What kind of man had no wish to see his son?

"Was it so very terrible? Being married to him?" James surprised her by asking.

"At first it was dreadful. Father had me wedded within a month of your leaving."

"Did he treat you ill?" He turned in the seat to look at her.

"Not ill, precisely. Calder did not wish to be married to me any more than I did to him. Nonetheless, I tried to be a good wife."

James took her hand and squeezed it affectionately. "I am sorry for what you were obliged to go through."

"And I, you. I had no idea you would be sent away."

"Whoever would have thought the world existed beyond the two of us?" he asked sardonically.

"Sadly, we are as insignificant as two specks of sand upon the earth."

"Now that might be going too far. I am at least the size of a rock."

"You may be a rock, then..." She laughed. "...although I should prefer to be, at the least, a sapphire or ruby."

"Most certainly, ma'am. When I said rock, I believe I encompassed all types of rocks, including precious stones."

She leaned her head against his shoulder, relishing the warmth and comradeship which came so easily with him. "I think what I missed the most was your ability to make me smile. I have had little to smile about since you left."

"Except for Tommy," he added.

"Yes. Tommy saved me from despair." What had saved James, she wondered, but did not want to ask. No doubt his brethren had had the major part in that.

"James, do you think perhaps you would ride with me after everyone has left?" It was bold to ask, but she would regret it if she did not.

"Meet at the meadow the morning after?"

It was what he had been used to saying to her every day. Even knowing it was unwise, her heart leapt with hopefulness.

"Meet at the meadow."

CHAPTER 11

"What have I agreed to, Sancho?" James asked as he saddled the steed. "I know you will be pleased to see Morag. If only humans could be as simple in their dealing. 'I like you, do you like me? Very well, then,'" he mumbled aloud.

Sancho shook his head.

The goodbyes, made that morning, had been long, and James was glad to have them over with. In many ways, he felt as though he was once again shirking responsibility by allowing Waverley to take his parents south to one of his houses, but he also knew Waverley would not have offered were he not sincere. As he had said to the Duchess, the estate's repair, and seeing his family settled, would owe much of its haste to the Duke. Of course, Anna had been the one to assist Elspeth. He was very fortunate in his friends—not that he could attribute what had been done to his account.

He knew it was dangerous to become close to Anna again, but he could not help himself from licking up whatever crumbs she chose to throw at him. He still had nothing to offer her, but at least now he understood that. When he had been a lad of eighteen, he had been righteously offended and angry. Now, he was just sad for what might have been which could never be.

Out of habit, James rode up to check the fences on the way to the meadow. It was a beautiful afternoon so far, but in Scotland a storm could form over the mountain in what seemed like seconds. Hopefully, the weather would bless both families' trips south, and he fully intended to enjoy his time with Anna. There was a reason she wanted to meet, he suspected.

As soon as they breached the crest and began descending into the valley, Sancho's ears pricked up. Morag and Anna were already there, waiting for them, James thought, as Sancho stood taller and began to prance. "Do you think that really impresses her, old pal?"

Sancho brayed.

"I do know that making a noise like a donkey does not. Or does it? Should I start braying, too?"

Sancho snorted and continued his strange courtship. Soon, James saw Morag too, and therefore Anna must already be waiting under the tree.

When he saw her, he felt his resolve to remain aloof again begin to slip. She was still the most beautiful creature he had ever seen, sitting there on a blanket under the tree, with the lake behind her. It was a scene he had held close to his heart for a decade. It was a vision of the past, except he had enough awareness to know it was not the same.

It was, however, hard not to repine. Had her father allowed it, they would have been married ten years by now and have their own children.

"Anna," he greeted her as he slid from Sancho and removed his saddle and bridle.

James watched with amusement as Sancho and Morag cantered off together. "Does it seem to you as though we are arranging assignations for our horses?"

"Indeed it does. Come, sit down, James. Cook has prepared a veritable feast for us. Most of it, I suspect, is left over from the ball."

"Haggis?" he teased, drawing a laugh from her as he had hoped it would.

"Mother would be mortified if she knew the truth of it. I have sworn Cook to secrecy. 'Tis a pity we will never know if the Duchess liked it or not."

"I imagine I can discover that once I see her again. It did not occur to me to ask, during the rush of departure this morning."

"It matters little. I confess I am a little relieved to be alone."

James turned to look at her. "A spectre, am I?"

In return, she favoured him with a look of exasperation. "You are well aware of my meaning. Have you had any respite since the wars ended?"

"Some. Most of it on my journey here. I dreaded every step of the way, not knowing what I was facing or how I was to manage."

"And now? Are you sorry to have returned?"

He angled his head in thought for a moment. "No, I must admit things have turned out far better than I could have hoped. I cannot imagine Mr. Barrett will wish to stay here long, but I am grateful he has taken the reins to set things to rights."

"I rather think whether he remains or no will depend on Margaret and if she returns unwed or not."

"If she returns, I imagine he will be the reason. What else will there be for her here, with our parents now gone?"

Anna did not answer. Instead, she asked brightly, "Are you hungry?"

"Always," he agreed as she began rummaging through the hamper.

"Would you care for a chicken leg, perhaps?"

"My favourite," he remarked, even as she piled a small plate with several pieces of chicken, a plum and a bread roll before handing it to him.

They ate their fill, then James lay back on one arm while Anna put away the dishes and food.

She leaned back against the old oak and looked up at the sky.

"What do you plan to do next, Anna?"

"Must we think of that today?"

"I suppose not. I am merely curious. Surely you do not mean to stay here indefinitely? Did you not remark about wishing to be near to Tommy?"

"I did." She closed her eyes, so James watched her, admiring her beauty while she was unaware of his consideration. Her alabaster skin had always fascinated him. 'Twas in stark contrast to his own, which was now becoming lined from being so much in the elements. He had never taken much care to cover his face. It seemed a silly thing when one was fighting for one's life.

"The earldom has many properties. I have considered making one of the smaller ones my home—preferably one the Dowager Countess feels beneath her notice to visit."

"Is there one close to Windsor?"

"Yes, relatively close. Runnymede is not a far ride. It lies a little distance down the river. I looked the house over after I left Tommy at school."

"Why do you hesitate? It sounds perfect."

"I hardly know. Mayhap I am hesitant to go there alone. It is ironic, is it not, when I could not wait to have Kiernan to myself?"

"I understand. It is familiar here and you are not making a fresh beginning. People know you, the household is your mother's and therefore you need have no worries. When you move to a new house, and a new place, no one is familiar."

"You do understand, although, if truth be told, the main objection I have is it is still within the Dowager's purview."

"Even though she would not deign to reside there?"

"It is close enough to Radford for her to drop in unannounced."

"Ah. And therefore you consider she will still control the servants?"

"She would make the attempt, I know, but should I decide to remove there, I must not abide her interference. I must be sure to have anyone disloyal to me moved to another property."

"That would be wise," he agreed.

"The only place I am truly safe from her is Scotland. She thinks we are all heathens."

James laughed. "Are we not?"

She scowled at him in a playful fashion, making him feel more light-hearted than he had in some time. It was easy to forget his woes when he was with her. "What does she do that is so dreadful?"

"It is hard to explain. At first, she seemed quite helpful with her suggestions."

"But then they are not really suggestions, are they?"

"No. They are more like commands," she agreed.

"That is a situation I am quite familiar with. Did you notice how commanding Waverley was?"

"The two are not even comparable." She shook her head.

"Perhaps not in the delivery," he acknowledged. "I have not met the Dowager Countess, but if you think the Duke does not intend to command when he makes a suggestion, you are sorely mistaken. He has pulled the wool over your eyes!" He shuddered dramatically.

"Did you ever find him rummaging through your belongings, spying around corners or correcting everything you did?"

"I would call that freakish and controlling rather than command-ing. Have you ever asked her to leave you alone?"

"One does not ask the Dowager Countess of Calder anything of the sort."

"There must be something you can do other than hide in Scotland, surely?"

She shook her head slowly. "Nothing that I can think of, besides avoiding her as much as possible. I know I must go either to Runnymede or to London. I cannot return to Radford. Visits with Tommy will be required, of course, but I doubt I can bring myself to live there while she is still amongst the living." She glanced away along the peaceful valley. "I realize how shocking that sounds."

He ignored her last, sad statement. "There is nothing to be done short of matricide?"

Anna did not laugh.

"Perhaps," she said dolefully, "if I were to remarry... yet I am not even certain that would stop her from trying to control me—and Tommy."

"Then you must needs present it to her as an accomplished fact —*fait accompli* as they say."

"Yes," she whispered. *"Fait accompli."*

A{FTER THEIR FIRST PICNIC}, James and Annag spent time together every day. Some days they would ride, some days they would enjoy further picnics at the meadow. It was like old times, even though before, when she had been but a child, the days had been full of hope. Now, however, James seemed determined to be nothing more than her friend. If only she could guard her heart!

At least they were able to spend time together without anyone knowing. They could ride on their land or meet in between without causing gossip or damning suppositions.

She had never found the same ease of friendship with anyone else. Was it any wonder she had fallen in love with him?

The post came just as Annag was leaving to ride to the meadow, so she took the letters with her. Since she often arrived some time before James, she thought to read them while she waited. Before mounting, she packed them into her saddle bag, along with the cheese, fruit and elderflower wine Cook had prepared. The time for Annag to make a decision was drawing near—although there really was no decision to make, was there? This time of happiness was soon to draw to a close.

She dismounted and allowed Morag to graze while they waited. Eager to read the letters, she quickly unpacked and spread out a blanket woven in the McKiernan plaid of blues and greens to sit upon.

There was familiar script on each letter, so she chose to read the one from Tommy first.

Annag gasped.

"Why the long face? Have you had bad news?"

Annag lowered the paper. "I did not even hear you approach."

"Then it must be a fascinating letter. From Tommy, I conjecture?"

"Yes. He fell playing cricket and dislocated his shoulder." She was trying to remain calm.

James sat next to her and put his arm around her. "Do you want to cry?"

She nodded; her head had already drooped against his chest.

"Then cry. I will whisper nonsense to you about how these things happen and he will be quite well by now. Nothing I say will matter but you will feel better once you have wept."

"Oh, James. He is still so young to be away from home. Before I know it, he will be asking to spend the holidays at someone else's house and I do not know if I could bear that."

"I suspect you have a year or two before that happens."

He handed her a handkerchief and she blew her nose. Thankfully, she had cried most of her tears by the time he arrived and thus had not made a complete fool of herself.

"Have you read the others?" he asked, looking at the handful of missives on the blanket.

"Not yet. I opened Tommy's first."

"Of course," he agreed, as though it were the natural choice. "I had some letters today myself. One from Margo, one from my mother and another from Waverley, although they were all in one neat packet franked by the Duke."

"Is all well?"

"Yes, indeed. They have arrived in Bath and everyone seems pleased with the situation. Apparently behind the study, there are doors leading to a neat little gated garden and my father seems content to spend his time between the two."

"I am glad to hear that. And how does your mother?"

"She does not know what to do with herself. Waverley's servants are tending to her every need."

Annag smiled. "She will soon find some society. Bath is a small enough community that I am sure she will find ladies to befriend."

"Margo reassures me that Mother and Father are doing well. She went to London before they posted the letters. As expected, she is in awe of the ducal town house and the hustle and bustle of Town."

"I remember my first visit. I felt like a fish out of water. I am certain Margaret will be all the rage with her beauty and their Graces' patronage."

"I cannot say if she will enjoy that, but I am glad she has the opportunity all the same," he said reflectively. "Would you like me to leave you so that you may read your other letters?"

"Oh, by no means need you do so. They are from my mother and sisters. There will be nothing but humorous inanities in them."

"It still surprises me how much ladies can write. I find it difficult to fill a page even when I have something to say."

Annag shook her head as she reached for the letters. "This appears to be the oldest. I have little doubt my family forgets that the post takes a couple of weeks to arrive here. This one is from Fenella. Let us hope she behaves with more decorum in London then she did at our ball!"

"I would not count on it," James muttered.

Annag read a few lines to herself.

"I trust it is good news?"

"I thought you were going to allow me to read in peace. Very well, then."

My Dearest sister,

How I adore London! For the life of me I cannot imagine why you dislike it so. The shops alone are enough to make me squeal with delight! Between the three of us we purchased over twenty bonnets, pairs of stockings and gloves on our first day! The Duchess was kind enough to extend to us our first invitation, to their ball. They are hosting it in Margaret's honour! Why, they surely could have also held it on mine and Innis's behalf, could they not? She was not even coming to London at the outset! However, Mama says we will have many invitations after that and I should be grateful for the connection. There were several handsome cavalry officers riding in Hyde Park. I do so hope they will be at the ball to dance with me! La, but London is ever so much more exciting than Kiernan. I hope you are enjoying yourself in that stuffy, quiet place, even though I will never understand why you prefer to be there.

· · ·

Annag slapped the letter down on the blanket. "Oh, Fenella."

"At least she is not in trouble yet," James teased.

"That was but the first day! Give her time." Annag leaned back against the tree. "I do not know if I can read any more of her prattle at this moment."

James pulled an apple from the bag and handed it to her. "Eating will make you feel better."

"Cook told me she has sent some shortbread for you as well."

"She will have us all a stone heavier by Christmas," he remarked, though at the same time he eagerly pulled out the fresh biscuits and took a large bite of one.

"She enjoys fattening you and the other men. The two soldiers are but skin and bone according to her."

"I hope they can be happy here. At least they have purpose and the village seems to be accepting of them."

"If only they will allow that acceptance."

James then withdrew a flask of wine and pulled out the cork. He handed her the bottle and she took the first sip. It was the perfect combination of sweet and tart and paired flawlessly with the cheese he handed to her next.

"I wish things could stay this way forever," she said wistfully, gazing up at the clouds swirling across the sky. Even those were beginning to darken, signalling that her perfect afternoon was soon to be at an end. Part of her wanted to say more to James, but he had given her no sign, no hint, of wanting anything more from her. It would certainly make the next fortnight awkward if he did not feel the same way. Yet if she remained silent, she was not sure there would ever be another such opportunity to be together. To her it seemed as if her feelings must be glaringly obvious, but her mother had remarked many a time on how dull gentlemen could be. It was difficult to reconcile the James she knew with being so blind, since he must have lived by his wits on the battlefield. Perhaps he did know how she felt and he simply chose to ignore it in favour of friendship? Perhaps a 'fishing expedition' might be in order...

"James, do you plan to marry now that your affairs are in a way to being settled?" She would outdo Fenella for boldness! Nothing ventured, she reflected with only a moment of remorse, nothing gained.

He did, however, look rather taken aback by her question. Oh, dear.

"I have given no thought to marriage since ours failed to take place. I cannot see how I would be a more suitable catch now than I was then."

Silly, silly man.

"Are you going to read the remainder of your letters?" he suggested.

"Are you trying to change the subject?"

"Not even subtly."

"Very well." She held out her hand to accept the next letter from the pile he then handed her.

"From Mother," she said as she scanned the missive. "And no, I am not reading every word. She says little more than Fenella did." Annag tossed it aside and took the next. "Innis," she announced as she broke the seal and unfolded it. "She writes of spending time with Margaret and the Duchess." She scanned some more lines. "Margaret is the toast of the *ton* as we all predicted. She does say one soldier has been paying Fenella *excessive attention*. She underlined that heavily."

"I suppose that is good news, depending on who the officer is, of course. Though he may not be titled or wealthy."

"I expect there is more of the same in all of these." She tossed them aside.

"You should at least read them if they have taken the trouble to write them," he said in an off-handed manner.

"I will read them properly later and respond accordingly, but... I should tell you... I am enjoying spending the afternoon in your company."

She looked at him pointedly, willing him to kiss her. He seemed to be considering it as his eyes darkened and he glanced at her lips, but then he drew back.

"The village fair is on Saturday. Would you care to go with me?"

Trying to mask her disappointment, she forced a smile. "Of course."

CHAPTER 12

*J*ames had been about to kiss Anna and it would have been another disaster. He did not wish to shun her company, but being alone with her was akin to the forbidden fruit dangling within an inch of a starving man. The village fair would at least provide a hundred chaperones. Anna might be a little lonely, but nothing good could come from kissing.

The last few days most of the village had come to help with his harvest and he had seen Anna a few times in passing. Her cook had been kind enough to provide sandwiches for the workers and Anna had helped pass them out with jugs of ale.

Hopefully the days had given her time to be relieved they had not kissed. Soon it would be time for her to leave—he just had to be strong a little while longer.

Today he drove the cart, because truth be told, he hurt everywhere and even the idea of riding was painful. He had joined in the harvest alongside all of the men and could not remember the time he had ached so much.

The cart was not fancy like a countess would be used to, but perhaps reminding her of his poverty was prudent.

Surprisingly, Anna was waiting for him, so he pulled the horses to a halt and jumped down to help her in.

"Good morning," he said, trying not to notice how fresh and beautiful she was even in her more subdued day dress. Even so, she still stood out like a beautiful rose amongst the wildflowers. Lawks but he was becoming poetic.

"Good morning," she returned. "Are you hurt?"

"And here I thought I was doing an excellent imitation of walking normally. I hurt everywhere, but I am not injured, per se. All of those years of campaigning for naught." He climbed into the cart with a wince. "You may laugh." He noticed her trying to fight back a smile.

"At least the harvest is over with."

"Indeed, and we had a much better year than we expected. Not that it will pay down much of the debt, but at least the debt would not be deeper."

"See? There is a bright side."

"If you insist." He pulled to the side of the dirt road they were travelling on to allow a carriage to pass. The driver held up a hand of thanks.

"I do insist. Now what shall we do first?"

"Your choice. As small as it is, we will have time to do everything twice before luncheon."

"I seem to recall you excelled at the archery."

"Only because the other competition was elderly or juvenile."

"You are too modest. I am certain you excel at many things."

"No, my only talent here is eating soor plums."

"And yourself? You going to show all of them your prowess with a caber?"

"Perhaps I shall," she said with a wry smile. He liked that he could make her smile. But would that smile fade quickly when he could not provide the luxury she was used to? Or when she had to pay for gowns herself from her jointure? Talk about a lesson in humility having a wife that had to buy him things.

They pulled into the village green where everyone from the county had gathered. He handed the reins to the ostler at the inn, handed Anna down, then they walked the short distance to the green.

It was nothing like some of the larger ones he had seen in England, like Bartholomew's, that had circus performers, animals and fortune tellers. This was more like a church fete where there were baking contests, several homemade items, a little show of manly strength, and a great deal of drinking whisky. It was Scotland's favourite past time after all.

If the villagers were surprised to see he and Anna together, they did not show it. It was a cheerful scene with tents, games, music playing in the background and children chasing each other between the crowd.

"I do so enjoy the fair!" Anna said. "It might seem silly, but this was my favourite day of the year when I was a child."

"I could see why. I always enjoyed it myself," he agreed.

"I am surprised my family left before the fair, but Father was never much one for gaiety, and Fenella was likely driving him mad to go on to London."

They passed a crowd gathered around a man on stilts who was breathing fire at the same time.

"That seems rather idiotic," James remarked. "If he doesn't break his neck on the stilts, then he has a back-up means with which to injure himself."

Anna said, "I have never known you to be cynical."

"Stating facts is hardly cynicism," he protested.

They walked on to where the pies were about to be judged.

"Oh, Captain Frome! You are just in time!" Mrs. Croft exclaimed.

"Oh dear, you are about to be roped in to judging," Anna muttered.

"Since Laird McKiernan is not here, can you judge in his stead?"

"Of course, but you know I have never met a pie I did not love. I will not be able to choose!"

"Well even if you pick one blindfolded, you must," she insisted as a group of ladies stood nearby waiting nervously.

Mrs. Croft had already taken his arm and was leading him over to the table. There were at least twelve pies there. "I will be fatter than the biggest whale in the sea after this," he teased.

"Nonsense! You could use some meat on those bones. War has made you too lean," she said as she pinched his arm.

He smiled and sampled as good-naturedly as he could, trying to exclaim the excellence of each one, though they all began to taste the same after the first three.

"What is your choice, Captain?"

"I am afraid beef ale will always be my favourite though I am also partial to the venison and cranberry. See? I am a terrible judge! I like them all!"

The lady who baked the beef and ale exclaimed with delight, while he and Anna moved on to the puppet show where every child was enthralled with the Punch and Judy show. Punch was currently mistreating Judy, and Mr. Scaramouche was trying to intervene.

"Tommy loves puppet shows," Anna said as they stood at the back and applauded when Punch was caught and punished for his exploits.

"You will be seeing him soon." James was filled with sudden sadness. What would it be like when she left? He supposed he would befriend the steward and they would drink a lot of whisky together. A startling, maudlin realization.

"Yes, I suppose it is time to think about my new life," she seemed to feel as sad as he.

"Captain Frome!" the village blacksmith shouted, then waved James over. "We need another for the archery contest."

"Then you want Lady Calder, here," James offered.

"Nonsense, sir. They do not want ladies to best them," she teased.

"Well, I suppose if you need someone to be a loser, then I am your man. I have not used a bow in ages." That was not quite true as they had hunted by necessity when encamped. But neither did he intend to hit the centre of the target each time.

He stepped up and took his three shots which all landed respectively around the middle.

Joseph Campbell was a perfect shot hitting all three dead centre. The crowd cheered and James held out his hand to congratulate the man. "There never was anyone who could best you, Joseph. I am glad I was able to make you look even better."

"You are very obliging, sir," he returned the handshake.

"You should challenge Lady Calder. She might actually provide you some real competition."

"Why not?" Mr. Campbell looked over at Anna. "Would you care to have a turn?"

Anna smiled. "Just for fun? Why not?"

James' three arrows were pulled from the target and brought back to Anna. She tested the strength of the bow a couple of times before she positioned one of the arrows, pulled back and snapped straight to the centre.

"Bravo!" the crowd cheered. She repeated the effort two more times, then smiled grandly at James, then at Mr. Campbell.

"Very impressive, my lady," he said with a bow. "Shall we check the targets?"

"I think we shall call it a draw, Mr. Campbell. Thank you for allowing me to participate."

She held out her hand to the man and he seemed unsure at first but took it and shook it heartily.

"Why did you do that?" she asked as they stopped for some lemonade and drank it beneath the shade of the old oak.

He gave a little shrug. "I thought you would enjoy it. You were always the better of us."

"That is not what I meant, and you well know it. You deliberately missed the centre. It was because of the five guinea prize, James."

He wagged his eyebrows. "Maybe, maybe not."

She shook her head. "You are a good man, James."

ANNAG COULD NO LONGER fool herself that she did not want James. He was pushing her away—she could feel it—and time was running out to convince him.

They finished their lemonade and watched as some of the young ladies were performing a maypole dance with bright, streaming ribbons.

It was hard not to reminisce when she saw the young girls who were about the same age she had been when she had first fallen in love with James. In fact, they had attended this village fair together that summer, but he did not seem to remember... or chose to forget.

They clapped along with the crowd that had gathered to watch the girls perform when they finished. They were all smiles and giggles and rosy cheeks.

"What would you like to do next? I told you we would be done by noon."

"We have not been to all of the vendors, nor the bagpipes and then there is always the dance and bonfire later in the evening."

"I beg your pardon!" he said as though he had not attended the fair every year of his life until he left for the army.

She was called upon to judge the quilts, then he threw a very respectable caber—to lots of admiring glances and whistles from the village women—in his shirt sleeves. She could not blame them.

They purchased some cheese scones and settled in to watch the local regiment dance to the bagpipes. What was left of the local regiment.

Annag sat next to James on the side of the hill. He seemed distant all of a sudden and she was not sure why. She chewed in silence and listened to the haunting, mournful song of the pipes. Perhaps that was what changed his mood? She stole a glance at him and indeed, he seemed to be blinking away tears. He swallowed hard.

She reached over and took his hand and gave it a comforting squeeze. There was nothing romantic in it, but he was many miles away and something was causing him pain.

Her hand must have brought him back to the present. He looked at her for a moment, still lost in time, before he recalled himself.

"Forgive me. I forgot that the last time I heard this music was the night before Waterloo."

The night before the wretched battle that had finally defeated

Napoleon. But at a great cost. England and Scotland alone had lost thousands of men.

"The Gordon Highlanders performed some reels at the Duchess of Richmond's ball. Then were dead the next day."

Annag felt goosebumps all over hearing his haunted story. "Oh, James, I am sorry. I cannot imagine what you have seen."

"Or what I have done," he said under his breath, but she heard.

They watched the remainder in silence, the gaiety of the afternoon suddenly gone.

Even as the bagpipes left and were replaced by fiddles, Annag expected James to wish to leave. The clearing that had held the morose scene before them was suddenly replaced by lively country dancing.

"Shall we join them?" he surprised her by asking.

"I thought you might wish to leave."

"No, I wish to dance." He took her hand and lifted her indecorously to her feet. She laughed. How the dowager countess would have an apoplexy if she saw! With that thought for encouragement, they almost ran down the hill to join the growing number of revellers. James took her elbow and swung her around to the lively rhythm.

Mr. Barrett nodded to them as he swung a pretty young lady past them. Most of the eligible young ladies were waiting for a chance to dance with Mr. Barrett, and he seemed good-naturedly willing to oblige each of them a turn.

Annag felt sixteen again, except perhaps she was not as fit. There had been little dancing during her marriage. James appeared just as lost to the music as she. One would never know that he was near tears moments before. Perhaps this was necessary to push away the demons and memories from Waterloo… to keep on living lest those deaths be in vain.

She found herself laughing and dancing with abandon, at times barely able to stay on her feet. It was the most freedom she had felt in ten years. She might regret it later, though she did not think she would. She was still laughing and breathless when James escorted her from the dancing to a copse of trees in the shadows. As he leaned against a tree, she saw a slight grimace on his face.

"I forgot you were still sore from the harvest!"

"I was trying not to let it show. It is ungentlemanly to remark upon it." Always teasing, was James.

"You certainly had me fooled. I was trying to keep up with you. It was just like old times." She stared up at him and their gazes locked. She did not know whether her breathlessness and pounding heart was from dancing or from anticipation. Time seemed to stand still as decisions were made. Annag had known almost immediately after seeing him that her heart was still constant, but she could understand why he doubted. Still, she thought she might be able to convince him with a kiss. Boldly, she leaned forward and stood on her tiptoes. Soon her hands were on his chest and she could feel when he gave in. His hand caressed her cheek gently, reverently, and their lips met at long last.

Annag had wondered through the years if she would ever be kissed again. This was better than she remembered.

There was an instant rush of longing, aching, relief. She never wanted it to end. She wrapped her arms about his neck and deepened the kiss. James made a growling noise in his throat and pulled her closer, the abandonment from their dance seemed to have transferred to their kiss. Annag forgot where she was. She forgot everything but James. Nothing that felt so right could be wrong. They were meant to be together.

Pounding thunder broke into her consciousness, but she willed it to go away. But it was a rider galloping towards them causing James to pull back, the perfect moment gone.

The rider stopped before the crowd and dismounted, leading his horse. He stopped and spoke to the first people he saw, who pointed to the dancing, so he kept moving.

"Who do you think he is looking for?" Annag asked, though she still clung to James.

"I do not know, but I should find out. Chances are it is one of us. How many people could send a rider such as this?"

That much was true. The message must be urgent.

He disengaged himself and Annag immediately felt the loss. She looked around and it was a wonder they had not been seen. Instead of following after, she remained where she was to regain her senses. No doubt she looked as thoroughly kissed as she felt. James was fortunate to have a beard to mask, but that beard had also likely threatened her face. She touched the skin which was still warm from his embrace.

What would happen next? Surely James could not deny what was between them?

She took a deep breath and tidied her hair knowing she could not dither much longer. When she had her bonnet back in place and felt a little more composed, she turned to see where James had gone.

After scanning the crowd, she was able to locate James' ginger head above the crowd. She waited to see what happened, for a messenger simply delivered a message and left, did he not?

Her wait was not long. She saw the messenger nod and ride away again. The crowd that had gathered around parted, and James and Mr. Barrett approached. Something was wrong, she could tell by the look on James' face. Her heart plummeted to her toes.

CHAPTER 13

*J*ames' height was useful when looking for someone in a crowd. He spotted the rider on the periphery, who was waiting for someone to fetch Mr. Barrett from the dance. James reached him before Mr. Barrett did.

"Are you Captain Frome?" He nodded with familiarity to Barrett.

"I am."

"Your butler said I would find you here. I was asked to give this to you or Mr. Barrett from his Grace."

He handed James the note.

"This cannot be good." Many scenarios leapt through his mind, first and foremost that something had happened to his father. He broke the seal and unfolded the note.

LADY FENELLA IS MISSING. *Come at once. I have summoned everyone to help. Best to be on the lookout on your way south via Gretna.*

ANNA WOULD HAVE to be told, and he hated to ruin her holiday, but knew it was best to be frank.

He turned to the rider. "Please return to my estate and rest for tonight. Tell them I sent you."

"I am much obliged, Captain." The man bowed then remounted and headed away from the village. He and Barrett followed the man's path back to where Anna had been, reflecting on what had happened. How things had changed in a matter of minutes! He had been saved from making a grave mistake. Was it fate that had stopped where the kiss was leading? Would he have confessed more to her than he could give her?

"What is it, James?" He looked up. Both Anna and Mr. Barrett were looking on with worry.

"Lady Fenella has disappeared. Waverley has asked me to come at once."

"Is that all it says?" she asked.

James handed her the note. "I am afraid there is no other information. Do you think she ran away?"

She gave him an imperious look. "This is Fenella we are speaking of, though I would not have thought even she could be so, so..."

"Idiotic? Sancho and I can ride through Gretna and check there. If we leave soon, we can cover many miles today. I will send word as soon as I know something."

"Now who is being idiotic? I am coming with you." She threw up her hands then turned to walk towards the inn where the cart had been left.

"Anna, we must ride. It will be very long, hard days in the saddle." He followed as he tried to speak reason to her.

"This is my sister we are speaking of. I bear more responsibility than anyone else here. Had I gone I might have prevented this. My mother was always over indulgent with her, but still the shame it will bring! I have little doubt she brought this upon herself."

"Do not berate yourself. It will do no go good. I have learned over the years that one intent on folly will find folly. But we do not know that is what occurred here."

"Do you think she was kidnapped?"

"I know no more than you, but it would be foolish to make too many assumptions."

"Shall I come too, Captain?" Mr. Barrett asked. James had forgotten the man was there. He stopped and turned to him. "Now that the harvest is done, it would be all right for me to leave for a time. Gilroy and Dunlap are capable of looking after things for a time."

"I very much appreciate your offer, but I think having someone here would be prudent. What if she returns here?" James did not think that likely, however. "I might have to send for you later if you are still able."

"Of course, Captain. I will go and begin making preparations." Mr. Barrett left. Anna was almost back to the inn so he hurried to catch up. Quickly they were on their way back to the castle.

"I will meet you at the intersection in an hour. We should start as soon as we can."

"You are certain?"

"I am going with or without you, James."

"There will be no luxuries, Anna," he warned. "We only stop when we can go no longer and sometimes sleep in less than salubrious environments. Sancho and I even spent a night in a barn along the way when we could find nothing else."

"I understand. None of that matters when my sister's welfare is on the line."

"How many miles have you ever been in a day?"

"Twenty? Perhaps more? I will not hold you back, James. Had we married, I would have experienced following the drum."

James did not know what to say to that. The thought of her in most every environment they had been in made bile rise in his throat.

"Pack lightly. Only what will fit in one saddle bag and save the other for food. We will have to stop to rest and water the horses on occasion, but Sancho is used to long hard rides. If he has not become too lazy here, that is."

"I will change horses if necessary," she remarked calmly. "I will not be deterred, James."

"Very well, I wanted you to know what you would be facing."

"It will not be easy and I will be fret with worry over my sister's welfare, but it must be done. I found I could do many things that were not pleasant over the past decade."

James felt like that was a gross understatement for him at least, but she was supposed to have been happy. His leaving was supposed to ensure that she made a good marriage unsullied by the likes of him. The old anger boiled his blood anew to know that she had suffered as well.

He drove the cart through the castle gates and soon they were at the front door. He assisted her from the cart then took off back to Alchnanny.

As he drove back to his estate, it was difficult to not think of the kiss. Had he completely lost his mind? He had been lost to sense of time and place and for those moments everything was Anna again. And for those few moments, he'd allowed himself to forget why they could never be. What if they had been seen? There would have been no choice but marriage and a lifetime of poverty for her. Had it not been for a decade of soldierly instincts to keep him alive, he would not have heard the rider approaching. The irony was, he was saved from one disaster only to be faced with another. He had little hope of finding Fenella untouched or unharmed, but she still had to be found.

James suspected Anna was hoping for much more. Of course he wished he had something to offer her, but it would be years—if ever—before his estate was flush with the world. However, he has suspected she did not really understand or think that it mattered. Therefore, this unplanned trip would be torture. They were searching for a needle in a haystack and James knew he and Anna would be closer than ever. Closer in proximity than they had ever been ten years before. A French prison would be less painful.

When he reached the stables, he explained the situation to Gilray, who understood the urgency and promised to prepare Sancho after he took the cart. James marched back to the house, already beginning to plan the route in his mind.

Once his bags were packed, he carried them out to the stables. He prayed heavenward for one last miracle, and then attached the bags to

Sancho's saddle. "Why Sancho? As if seeing Anna every day was not torture enough, now I will be with her all day long." Sancho turned his head to look at James, as if curious. "I am afraid you are going to come out of retirement to ride hard again for a few days. None of our lazy meandering like last time. At least you will have Morag to accompany you. I assume she will bring her."

About an hour later, he and Sancho were packed down with food and clothing, waiting for Anna at the designated meeting point south of the village. "It feels like old times again, Sancho. While I am not grateful for Lady Fenella's disappearance, I suppose it will be nice to have something to do other than watch the soil be turned over and planted."

Sancho stomped his hoof.

"Have patience, old fellow. She will be here soon." While he waited, he pulled out the map. It was not as though there are many choices of travel towards Gretna, but it was an old habit. Better the devil he knew. Just like the temptation he was about to face.

ANNAG SURPRISED JAMES by being on time. She had surprised herself, but she had never been one to waste time nor be late.

Despite her earlier protests to him, she had no idea how difficult the ride would be or if she had any notion of how to pack for such a trip, but she looked to have about the same amount of load as he. James joined her in a canter as she caught up with him. Thankfully Sancho and Morag seemed to appreciate they needed to hurry and as soon as they cleared the village, they trotted alongside each other at a decorous pace.

"I confess I am impressed."

"Impressed that I made the appointed time?"

"Yes, I suppose, but also you seem to have packed everything into the small bags."

"You expected me to have gowns thrown across the saddle and hanging from the bags?" She did not hide her amusement.

"I do not know what I expected, but here you are."

"I confess I will not be in the latest mode, but hopefully I will not hinder your progress either. James, I appreciate you going to help. It is my sister after all, and who knows how many days she has been gone by now. I do not know how much help we will be, but I could not stay home and do nothing."

"We might be more useful than you think. Hopefully she is simply having a lark and we find her unharmed."

"I wish I could even consider that an option. If she went willingly, then I have little doubt she thought it would be a lark. I think the very least of what might have happened is Fenella eloped."

"If that is the case, then our hunting might be very short indeed."

"How long will it take to get to Gretna?" she asked. "Do not coddle me, either. I may not be as long in the saddle as an old soldier, but riding was the only way to pass time for me these years."

"Very well, if we ride hard and cut across fields where we can, we might be able to make it by nightfall. But we have no indication how long she has been gone or who she might have left with. Did she have a very big dowry to tempt someone into such foolhardiness?"

"I would not think large enough to tempt a true fortune hunter, but I should think it similar to mine."

"Thousands of pounds at the very least."

"Yes," she agreed. "Father has always been frugal and did not waste away his money on anything frivolous like racing or gaming… or mistresses."

James looked over at her at that last remark. "Is that what your husband did? Has he wasted your fortune? Anna, are you in debt? Or should I say, is your son?"

"No, forgive me for making it sound that way, but certainly a good amount of money was wasted on such things. I have a handsome jointure so you need not worry."

He nodded, though appeared deep in thought. They sped up for a few miles as they cut across some open fields and had no traffic to contend with. This part of the lowlands was quite barren and beautiful. She was grateful it was still summer though or it would have been much harsher. It was hard not to imagine the worst of what was happening to Fenella, even though Annag hoped no harm had come to her.

James interrupted her thoughts. "Did you read the other letters? They might have given you a clue of someone she was particularly interested in or who was paying her marked attention."

"I did. The same thing had occurred to me. She mentioned several gentlemen, in fact. I know little of any of them. I remember one name in particular because he was a soldier. I thought you might know of him."

"It is a possibility, I suppose. Who is it?"

"Major Bexley."

James cursed under his breath, but she heard. "If there was one name out of all the army that was synonymous with gamester, cheat, womanizer, and scoundrel, it is Bexley."

"James?" she asked with worry.

"Let us pray it is not he. No wonder Waverley had sent for the brethren. They had every right to worry if Bexley was involved."

"What do you mean, James?"

"He has a history with innocent maidens."

Annag gasped. "What do you mean, James? What has he done?"

She could tell James was reluctant to say, but he did. "It is rumoured he ruins them and then demands a price for his silence."

"Why is he still a free man, then? One would think an irate father would have done something! Demanded marriage at the very least!"

"Unfortunately, many of the occurrences happened while we were on campaign. Often we had moved on by the time we had heard anything."

"So Wellington knew and did nothing?"

"I am certain he spoke to him about it, but by that point, we were gone, there was no proof—he claimed no force was necessary, and Wellington unfortunately had to leave discipline up to the brigade commanders. If he had to discipline everyone himself, then he would not have any time for military matters."

"So he is free to ruin my sister," she said angrily.

"It would appear so, yes. He is also one of the best cavalry officers that England has," he prefaced.

"So everyone looked the other way while he ravaged sweet, innocent young girls? How could Fenella be so stupid?"

"Bexley is quite handsome and charming. I could see easily how it would happen."

"James," she warned. She was in no mood for humour right now. "So he uses them, demands money and then disappears?"

"It is what his history has been. I am unaware of what his plan will be now. Perhaps he plans to return to the Continent. I do not know if he sold out or is only home on leave."

"I imagine he thought there would be little repercussions of dallying with an unknown Scottish lass." Annag felt sick. She could easily see how Fenella would be easy prey.

"If it were he, then I have little doubt he is unaware of the power behind your sister. He has had a run-in with the brethren before, and I assure you he will run for his life if he realizes we are after him."

"He deserves to be drawn and quartered. No, that is too good for him! Whether he harmed Fenella or not."

"I cannot disagree with you. If he survives this, I shall be very surprised. At the very least, he will not be welcome on British shores again."

Annag could not feel comforted by his words, though no doubt Bexley had picked the wrong prey this time. Who knew what he had already done to her by this point? They were forced to slow then stop by a herd of sheep crossing a narrow path. Sancho pawed at the ground as though irritated, mimicking Annag's sentiments. James conversed with the horse and he settled a bit. They must be over halfway to Gretna, and she was anxious to reach there that night, even though she doubted very much that Bexley would have marriage in mind. There was still a chance Fenella could have eloped with someone else, so it was worth looking there in case. What a disaster and change of fortune in the blink of an eye! It was hard to believe she had been so happy just a few hours before!

"Do you need to stop for a rest?" James asked, looking at her with concern.

"No," she shook her head. "I am still just filled with unbelief. I want to make it to Gretna tonight."

As if echoing her wishes, Sancho brayed at the herd with impatience. The shepherd finally looked up as if he had not noticed them before now and raised his staff in greeting.

"I envy the man his contentedness, but I do not think counting sheep will ever be mine," James remarked.

Annag wished she knew what would. She wanted to be his contentedness, his future. But now was not the time to think of herself.

It was twenty minutes before the herd passed and they could move on. It had felt like two hours. As they sped to a trot again, Annag was already beginning to grow saddle sore. It was going to be a long several days to London, but she refused to complain or give in this early. She would do what she could to find her sister, and there was nowhere else she would rather be than with James.

CHAPTER 14

*A*bout an hour before they reached Gretna, sheets of rain greeted them as daylight fell to dusk. By the time they reached the village, they were soaked all the way to the bone. When they reached the stables at the inn, and James helped Anna to dismount, her legs nearly buckled beneath her. She was shivering with cold.

"Why did you not tell me you were so bitterly cold?" he scolded with concern.

"I am well enough, James. There was no point in saying anything before now. There was nowhere we could have stopped."

A stable boy came running to take Sancho and Morag. "Please give them an extra portion of oats each. They will probably be happiest stabled together."

"Aye, sir," he said, accepting a coin. "See you to your missus. There be no need to fret about yon fine 'osses. I'll take good care of them."

Anna had removed her saddle bags and James quickly took them from her. "Take my arm."

"Do stop fussing, James. The blood has returned to my legs and I have no doubt I will soon be warming myself in front of a fire."

"Take my arm anyway."

Once inside the King's Head, the common room was full of people eating and drinking. James set down their bags and led Anna to the fire.

"May I help you, sir?" the innkeeper asked.

"Two rooms, if you please. A warm meal and a bath would also be welcome."

"Of course, sir. A hot meal is ready now—if a simple mutton pie and vegetables will suit you? I will have a bath sent up as soon as may be."

James looked over to Anna who nodded her agreement.

"Follow me, then, lad. I will show you to your rooms so your missus may change into dry clothing, and your food will be brought up straight away."

James did not correct the man. It was the logical assumption that he was travelling with his wife, but thank God that there had been two rooms available. He did not need that temptation.

He escorted her upstairs; at least her shivering had ceased, he noticed with relief.

A servant had already placed their bags in the two bedchambers, which were connected by a small sitting room in between, which held a table with two chairs and a small sofa near the fire.

"Your dinner will be brought up shortly," the man said as he closed the door behind them.

"We should change out of our wet clothing," he said.

"Yes," Anna agreed, went into the other room and closed the door. James made quick work of stripping off his wet garments and by the time he was in the sitting room the servants were already laying out their meal.

James thought it was a good opportunity to start asking questions, in the grim hope that it was not Bexley who had absconded with Fenella. He had seen no sign of either in the dining parlour, but he had not expected to.

"Have you, perchance, happened to see a young lady with bright red hair recently?" he asked a serving wench with a mop of black curls barely contained by her cap.

"Nobbut three or so just today, sir."

"Ladies? With bright red hair?" He did not trouble to hide his disbelief.

"Aye," she agreed as she set their places.

"I had not thought it such a common circumstance."

"Red hair? In Scotland?" She looked at him sideways and shook her head. "And it is not as if anyone uses their actual names in the register here, neither."

"I did," James muttered. "Would you perhaps have noticed a military gentleman? She would have been in the company of a cavalryman."

She shook her head. "That I would have remembered. But I would ask Mr. Elliott. He is the landlord here, but he considers himself the 'sole and only' parson in Gretna, though there be two others. Not all as weds stays overnight here."

"I am sure you are right. Thank you." The maid bobbed a curtsy then quietly left the room. James poured two glasses of wine while he waited for Anna.

"WHO WERE YOU SPEAKING TO, JAMES?" Anna asked as she came from her bedchamber. To his surprise, she was wearing a dressing gown and her hair down around her shoulders. The intimacy of it was almost too much to bear.

"I hope you do not mind that I have not dressed for dinner. Since the bath you ordered should arrive soon it seemed foolish."

"I do not mind," he said, trying not to look at her too closely. "I can have no excuse for objection when I am in my shirt sleeves, for which I beg your pardon." He held out his arms to display his equal casualness—but it was not equal at all. She was ravishing in the simplicity of her attire.

"What were you saying to her, if I may be inquisitive? It sounded to be more than a simple conversation."

"I was asking if she might have seen Fenella. Not by name, of course, but a red-headed young lady, perhaps with a military gentleman."

"You had no luck, I gather?" she asked as she served herself some pie and vegetables.

"Nothing."

"Is this the only place to look?" she asked. "I did not see many inns as we rode through the village, but it was raining rather heavily."

"The maid suggested we start with Mr. Robert Elliott. He claims to be the sole parson, though there are two others."

Anna nodded. "You should know I did not expect to find them here after what you told me about Bexley. It must be he."

James reached across the table and took her hand before he thought better of it. "Do not give up hope yet."

"It is difficult to see how any good may come of it. Our best hope was to find her here."

"I know."

"They could be anywhere."

"I assure you, Waverley knows Bexley well. If the culprit was indeed he, Waverley will, by now, be hot on his heels if not steps ahead."

"I wish I could have your faith. Poor Innis will have no chance of making a good match now."

James could hardly refute her statements. In all likelihood she spoke the truth. "The best thing we can do now is rest. I will make enquiries of all of the priests tomorrow and hopefully will by then have received some word from Waverley."

"I just wish we had more information!" She threw up her hands. "Surely they must have more information by now that we do not know?" she demanded. "Could they have found her already?"

"Waverley will send a message when he knows something. Recollect we received word earlier today."

"Was that really today? It is hard to countenance."

"It has been rather a full day, has it not? Your bath should be ready now. They have been filling it all the while. You should sleep well after that."

"I trust you may do so yourself."

James hoped he would be able to sleep after the long ride, but Lord knew his mind was contrary when he had much to occupy it, and with Anna nearby, there was always something troubling him. And, not to be dismissed, was the problem of Fenella. Even though she was a very silly girl, the thought of her in Bexley's clutches made James ready to commit murder. Anna had asked why had they not stopped him before. He wished he had had a better answer than the man was a good officer—on the field, that was. Sadly, much had been overlooked because of his abilities during the desperation of battle.

"James?"

He looked at Anna, not realizing his thoughts had led him to another place.

"Would you like to bathe when I have finished? You rode as long and hard as I."

"No, I will use the pump outside." *The cold, numbing pump, please God.* "I will see you in the morning."

"Rest well, James."

Before he could turn away, she stretched up and kissed him on the cheek, making him long to gather her in his arms. Instead, he patted her on the shoulder and then turned to escape to his room.

He was a coward for not having mentioned the kiss at the fête, but it seemed hardly the time, given the news of Fenella, and hopefully Anna would realize such an embrace could not happen again.

ANNAG CLOSED the door behind her and leaned against it, taking a long, steadying breath. A steaming hip bath was waiting for her and she sank into it with blessed relief. The muscles that were tight gave up some of their tension, though she knew another long day in the saddle on the morrow would feel like a thousand knives stabbing at her. However, she would not complain. *Consider James! This has been his life for a decade.* No, she could survive a few days with good humour. If only there were news of Fenella, then she would be able to enjoy these few days with James. She could already sense his reticence —and perhaps regret—for their kiss. The proximity and sharing of a parlour—even dining together—was more intimacy than she had had with her husband. James already treated her with more kindness and affection than Calder had throughout the entirety of their life together. It was hard not to wish for more.

Calder would not have lifted a finger to help Fenella, yet James and his brethren had all put aside everything at a moment's notice in order to help.

It was hardly the time to be making comparisons or dreaming up romantic notions, but Annag also knew she had limited time in which to convince James. The question was, how?

She pondered this until the water grew cold, but by the time she had climbed into bed and closed her eyes, she had no more idea than at the beginning. After that glorious kiss, she knew he was not indifferent to her, but James' honour was too great and she understood he felt the gap in stations to be too wide to provide for her in the manner to which he believed she was accustomed. If only he could understand that all she wanted, after her unhappy marriage, was to be loved. She had everything that money could buy, but happiness was free. Pride was a devilish thing.

THE NEXT MORNING, she was as sore as she had expected to be. She slid her feet onto the floor and stretched, willing the muscles to move, but they were howling their protest. She dressed again in her riding habit of green corduroy—thankfully it had dried in front of the fire during the night—then brushed her hair and pulled it into a simple knot at the back of her head.

James was already in the sitting room, enjoying a cup of coffee. He was writing a letter to someone while the maid was finishing setting out their breakfast.

"Good morning. Is there any news?" she asked, aiming for a bright tone.

"Not yet," he answered, standing at her entrance and helping her to sit down at the table. "You find me penning a note to Waverley, but I will wait until we have verified there has been no wedding here before I send it."

"I was hoping we would have heard something by now."

"I expect something soon. A messenger would have to trace our movements, after all. In fact, on that note, I do not think it prudent to move from here until we do. That is why I was preparing my report, in order to send it back with his servant."

Annag hated being idle—it was the reason why much of the past decade had been untenable. Her sister was alone somewhere with an unknown rogue and Annag could do naught but wait.

"Come, let us eat and then we will walk to visit the church," he said, seeming to understand her inability to do nothing.

The fare provided was hearty, with eggs, sausage, black pudding, and tattie scones. She was surprisingly hungry and cleared her plate.

Once satisfied, they walked into the village. The church was a brown stone building, but their search was unfruitful. No one recognized their descriptions of Bexley or Fenella, and their names were not in the register.

After no luck at the church, they went on to the blacksmiths. They knocked, and the young maid who opened the door held her finger up to her lips, indicating them to be quiet. "There is a wedding happening now," she whispered. Despite that, she let them in. A large anvil sat at one end of the room, and the blacksmith was wearing his apron, as if he carried on with his business in between weddings. Perhaps he did. It should not have been romantic, but somehow it was. Even in the small room that smelled of dirt and metal and was overly hot from the fire, there was something about it that was charming. Annag and James stood back in the shadows while the short ceremony was performed. The groom smiled with glee and picked up his young bride and gave her a loud, smacking kiss. They waited while the register was signed and some type of certificate was written and presented to them.

"Are those legitimate?" James leaned over to ask Annag.

"They must be or why would anyone worry about Gretna marriages? Why would people trouble to come all the way here?"

"That did not seem to be a very authentic ceremony," James responded with an adorable frown.

"You know as well as I do that in Scotland handfasting is a tradition as old as time. At least they receive a marriage certificate from this one."

"I daresay," he muttered, although he did not look convinced.

"I would never have taken you for an old-fashioned romantic, James."

"You think me romantic simply because I would prefer my wedding to be in a church, performed by an ordained priest?" he asked, his eyes wide.

"Yes. I must assume, then, that such principles mean I will not convince you to wed me at this moment." She teased only partially.

"Good morning to you, my lord, my lady," the blacksmith greeted them as he walked forward. Annag had not even noticed that the other couple was leaving.

"If you will step over here, I have a few questions you must answer before I can perform the ceremony, though I can see you are both of age."

"I beg your pardon, but there is a misunderstanding. We are not come to be wed," James explained.

"Ah, so ye be already wed, are ye? Well, then, how may I help ye?"

James cast Annag a rueful grin.

"We are looking for my sister, sir. We fear she may have been brought here against her will."

He rubbed his chin. "Of a surety I would remember someone as pretty as you, my lady. I have not seen anyone who came even close."

"Her hair is a little lighter and her smile..." Annag waved her hand in front of her face. "It is, shall we say, perhaps a little more..."

"Toothy?" James offered.

Annag nodded. "Yes, that is the word." She had been about to say more equine, but that would have been unkind.

"I hate to disappoint you, but still the answer is no."

"A young and giggly chit?" James tried. "Perhaps a few days ago? We are sadly lagging behind since we have come from south of Edinburgh."

"They often be disguised, you know, but I do have everyone sign my register. You are welcome to look through it. Most leave their real names there so the marriage is binding. I will nae marry anyone under age, nor without their consent."

"Very admirable," James said. "I am sure," he added on under his breath.

Despite her anxiety, Annag found herself smiling and began to turn the pages of the register.

"If you have no objection, my lord, I will leave you to your search. I have work to be doing between ceremonies."

"Not at all," Annag assured him as she continued to scan the register. "Do you think she might be in disguise? I cannot but feel such a ploy to be most unlike Fenella. She would give herself away in seconds."

"Should her name be in the register, then I very much doubt you will find Bexley's. He cannot have changed his colours so quickly since last I knew him."

Yet, as Annag scanned through pages and pages, she recognized neither names nor script which could be her sister's.

"Who would have thought there were so many clandestine marriages?" James asked with disbelief.

"I do not think she has come here, James."

"I was not really expecting to find her here, but I am glad we came."

They thanked the smith for his assistance then walked back to the inn.

"A messenger has arrived for you, sir. He is waiting in the parlour," the landlord informed James.

"Thank you," James said, with a knowing look at Annag.

The messenger stood up and handed him the note. He was the same man who had delivered the message to them at Galashiels.

"Thank you. I was not expecting to see you again so soon," Annag said.

"His Grace has several of us stationed at various places about the country, ma'am, and we each of us hand the messages on to the next on the road."

James nodded and explained, "We employed a similar relay service in the army. It keeps the horses fresher." Turning back to the messenger, he said, "I will return with a reply in a few minutes."

James then escorted Annag up to their rooms, and she was near to bursting with anticipation by the time he had closed the door behind them and opened the letter.

"What does it say?"

He ignored her while he read the letter to himself.

"You need not protect me, James. I have already imagined the worst."

"He says that he does indeed believe Bexley to be the man she is with, but thus far they have no other clues. He says Bexley's family estate is near where Thackeray lives, so he is searching there. Waverley has men searching through London. They have already searched all the roads leaving London and discovered no trace of them, so he believes they are still in the capital. Should we have found no trace of them either, he suggests we come on to London."

"It has been several days now. Has Bexley not asked for money?" Annag sounded impatient.

"He will wait until she is truly and utterly ruined. Waverley also mentions they have put it out that Fenella is nursing a cold, but that will only fadge for so long."

"Bexley must not intend to remain in England or he would not have done such a thing!"

"I cannot imagine what his motives are. Very likely he thought she had no one to protect her." James sat at the small table to finish his note. "Are your bags packed?"

"Yes. The maid saw to it."

"Then we should be on our way as soon as I have finished this."

"Should we trouble with a message when we are to travel to London ourselves?"

"The messenger will reach him much faster. You would be astonished by how swiftly the relay works. Even riding, we will travel far slower, especially if we are to keep Sancho and Morag."

"I would like to."

"In that case, my lady, I shall be ready to depart in a few minutes."

CHAPTER 15

*N*ever had James imagined he would be returning to London so soon. He did not mind the large city, except he did not precisely feel as if he belonged. What a strange thing to say in a city with a million people, yet while he was not really a member of the *ton*, he associated with people who were. When he was not in London, he did not think about it, because it really did not matter and it had not mattered when he was in the army. A battlefield was a great equalizer.

As they travelled to London with urgency, he found himself less and less resistant to Anna's charms. Being very near to her every day seemed so natural, so right, that it was easy to pretend the charade was real. When the two of them were alone, Anna did not behave like a high and mighty countess. In fact, she seemed very content in their meagre means of travel and had not once complained about the less than ideal conditions.

"Would you care to tell me why the brown study?" Anna asked from beside him as they slowed to a trot to enter a town.

"Why do you think that?"

"You have a certain look on your face," she said, waving a hand in front of her own. "Do you care to tell me what it is that has you so absorbed?"

"Not on this occasion." On no account should he speak aloud what he had been thinking. Some things were most definitely better kept to oneself.

"Hmm. Maybe I will tease it from you later."

On leaving Gretna, they had only travelled as far as Penrith the first day, but James knew there was little in the way of accommodation until Boroughbridge, so they had stopped for the night and were just now reaching the town on the third day. The messenger in Gretna had given him the locations where the messengers awaited each other, so he sought out the posting inn hoping there was more news from Waverley. James saw to the horses while Anna found a place to refresh herself. When he asked for her in the inn, he was shown into a parlour where she was waiting with a small meal already laid out.

"You are an excellent travelling companion. I could become accustomed to such service."

"I am enjoying it more than I expected. After a decade of tedium, this is quite an adventure. If I could but be certain my sister is safe, I would enjoy it more."

"Indeed. The innkeeper was busy, but I asked him to discover if there were any new messages awaiting me. He said he would check and bring them directly."

He nearly drained the mug of ale that Anna had thought to order for him. It was dangerous indeed, having someone be familiar with your partialities and order them without asking.

They had a simple meal of mutton stew and bread but it was filling nonetheless. The innkeeper came in with a new mug of ale. "Your pardon, sir. I have no message for you."

"Thank you," James replied.

"So we press onward," Anna said. "I know you have been considerate of me, James, but I would like to go as far as we can today."

"Very well. There will be better choices of accommodation now that we have gained a main road."

Anna nodded absently.

"What are you thinking?" he asked, noting her distraction.

"If I tell you, will you tell me?" she asked coyly.

"Absolutely not."

"How unfair you are, James. I was wondering what will become of Fenella. I would not wish her to be forced into marrying such a vile creature, but she will be ruined if they do not wed."

"I have long thought it grossly unfair how ladies receive such rough justice when such travesties occur."

"She might have gone willingly, but it seems wrong to be punished for life for being drawn into a spider's web. For all her silliness, she is not malicious."

"You are assuming Bexley could be brought to account... although Waverley could do it, if that was your wish."

"I think we need to know more first. Much though I should loathe to call him brother, it might be necessary."

"There could be stipulations, such as exile." He raised a brow in query.

"Do you mean for Fenella too?"

"No, probably not for her, but would Bexley allow her freedoms which are no longer his?"

"Such consideration is no doubt unlikely if his character is as black as it seems," she conceded.

They had both finished their meals and James pushed back from his chair. "If you are sufficiently refreshed, shall we continue?"

"Yes. We could stay at Radford tonight if you so wish. It is not far from Doncaster. The Dowager will be in London for the Season."

Knowing how much she seemed to dislike the place, James was surprised she would make such an offer. He did not really care to go anywhere that made him think of the late Earl and what her life must have been like with him.

"Only if you wish," he answered instead of voicing his thoughts.

"In all honesty, I would rather not inform the Dowager of my family situation—she would be bound to find out we stayed. It would only reinforce her low opinion of me and all things Scottish."

"On the other hand, it might be amusing to shock her by bringing your common Scottish male friend to the family estate... with whom you are travelling alone." He wagged his brows at her.

Anna laughed. "I find myself greatly tempted when you put it that way, but perhaps we should keep to the main road to make the best time."

Morag and Sancho were brought out ready for them and James helped Anna into the saddle. Even though she was putting her dirty boot in his gloved hand to be lifted, when she brushed by him with her scent of honey and lemon soap, he wanted to pull her down into his arms and kiss her senseless. He felt barbaric for even thinking such thoughts, but it was hard to pretend indifference when he felt anything but.

They kept their pace slow as they manoeuvred between loaded wagons, beer drays and private carriages on their way through the town.

"James?" Anna asked.

"Yes?"

"I would like you to meet Tommy."

"I would be honoured," he answered, even though he thought it would be torture to meet Anna's son by another man—a son that should have been his.

"Truly? I know it is a great deal to ask of you, but I would like him to have someone to look up to."

"As a father?"

She had the grace to blush, which even her bonnet did not hide on her porcelain skin. "He has no one else, besides elderly uncles. One of his favourite amusements is to play with his toy soldiers. I know he will adore you."

"Surely there is some gentleman more appropriate than I?"

She was shaking her head. "No, James, you are precisely the kind of gentleman he needs."

James nudged Sancho and picked up speed when they reached the open road. He was grateful for the need to change pace because he did not know what to say.

He had only to stay strong for a couple more days, he told himself.

Once Anna was distracted with the search for Fenella and back in the bosom of her family, she would forget about him. If she went into Society, no doubt someone worthy of her would offer her a more suitable life. Not that anyone was worthy of her, but she seemed as though it was her wish to remarry and find a father-like figure for Tommy.

Already James hated the man.

THEY WERE PUSHING the pace hard now that they were on the open road, and Annag knew their time together would soon be coming to an end. It would have been a horrible journey to have endured alone. Despite the poor circumstances, she would be forever grateful for the extra time she had been given with James. Even if he could never give her more of himself beyond this week together, it had been a rare gift.

Nevertheless, she was very sore from the saddle and did not know if her body would ever be the same. She supposed one must become used to it, but she did not know how soldiers and messengers rode for so long, day after day.

Annag said little more about Tommy during the rest of the journey, hoping that planting the idea in James' mind would be enough. He would be an excellent father, but would he mind the obligation? Annag supposed that she could have misread his character, but she did not think so. He had always been good with children when they were younger, and he knew that Calder had been no more of a father to Tommy than the provision of his seed.

The pretence of being James' wife was soon to be over. It had felt so right to her. Quite ignorantly, they had not discussed what would happen were they seen by anyone. Everyone they had dealt with had assumed they were married, and they had gone along with the assumptions. She was a widow, so it was not as scandalous as if she were a young maiden without a chaperone, but she was still a woman of virtue and would be thought fast if it were known that she was travelling alone with James. Even though she desperately wished to be his wife, she would not want him to offer under duress. He would feel obligated to protect her name.

They had made good progress south, but Morag threw a shoe when they were just to the north of St. Albans, forcing them to stop unexpectedly. James escorted her to the door to seek a private parlour, while he arranged for her horse to be re-shod. It was a very busy posting house and almost everyone coming and going from London passed through there. There were no private rooms available, so she was forced to sit at a table in the common room, which was crowded with travellers.

Annag had not troubled to be careful—it had not seemed necessary, or likely that they would run into acquaintances. It could have happened anywhere, of course, but the odds were certainly against them in a place like this.

When Annag had told James that Tommy needed a father in his life, she had not spoken lightly. The Dowager and Tommy's trustees would leap at the chance to remove Annag from any part in her son's upbringing. In fact, the man she saw across the room now had been the reason she had been separated from her child so soon. Her heart pounded in panic. She hated him, quite literally, and if he saw her now alone or with James, he would somehow use the fact against her, she knew it.

She put her head down, thankful she had not yet removed her bonnet. Had he realized she was there? His eyes met hers in a brief glance, his not seemingly with recognition. She had known him immediately. The man had made her life miserable since Calder's death, threatening to bring up her child himself. He had succeeded in separating her from Tommy by convincing the other trustees to send Tommy to school.

Annag would have to think of a story quickly. Perhaps she could fob him off if he came near, but what if James strolled up to her at the wrong moment? There would be no chance to warn him that The Honourable Archibald Radford was in the tap room and would ruin her if he knew they were travelling alone together. Why had she not properly considered? The answer was easy. Her first thought had been for her sister, which would also be used against her, and her second had been to rejoice at the chance of being with James.

Plausible stories raced through her panic-stricken mind. Perhaps it would be better simply to slip away and hide. James could return for food without her. Where could she go to be safe? The stable yard was hardly the place for a lady. Even in her plainest habit she would stand out.

The best answer was to find James and warn him, she decided. Otherwise, he would not know not to come in asking for her. It was difficult to see where Archibald had gone, but she doubted very much that he would remain in the tap room with commoners. She tried to peer around the room, but finding this impossible, decided it would be better to enlist some help.

THE ROOM WAS SO crowded it was a while before one of the barmaids came to ask Annag what she required.

Afraid to look up, Annag tapped her fingers on the table in agitation. The girl seemed to sense something was wrong, for she bent nearer under the guise of wiping the oak with the edge of her apron.

"Could you tell me if the large gentleman with the many-caped driving coat is still in here? He is quite tall and has silver hair."

The girl's body turned as she looked around. "There be someone by that description leaning against the bar, my lady, supping a pint of ale."

Annag could feel herself trembling. "Will you please help me? I must leave without him seeing me."

The girl hesitated.

"He is not my husband, but someone who wishes me harm nonetheless. It is a sad coincidence that we are both here at the same time." Annag pulled out a gold coin and set it carefully on the table.

The girl nodded. "There be a passage behind you near the kitchens. His back is turned, so you should find it easy enough to slip away, but keep your head down lest he turn this way."

"Thank you," Annag said, not knowing if she was heard over the din in the room.

"Wait for me beyond the door near the kitchen and I will help you more. Let me just tell my ma I have to step out."

Annag turned away from the bar where Archibald was—if the girl had spotted the right man. She kept her head down until she reached the door and was safely through. The small passage was dim and smelled of vegetables. There was a door on the other side, but she preferred to wait for her escort. Her knees shook as she waited; she expected Archibald to come thundering through behind her at any moment. She was being ridiculous, but if he knew the circumstances of her presence, he would not hesitate to publicly shame her.

Annag thought she must have been forgotten and hoped she could find James before he came looking for her. She moved from one foot to the other in agitation and debated venturing out on her own. She was just about to set forth in search of a door to the stables when the barmaid came through the door. "Begging your pardon, my lady," she said apologetically. "We be mortal busy today, we be."

"Can you point me in the direction of the blacksmith?" she asked the maid. "My horse threw a shoe and I would like to see if she is ready."

"This way." The girl opened the door and looked around cautiously before she motioned for Annag to follow. They were in the stable yard as she suspected and was grateful she was not alone, for some of the men made catcalls as soon as they saw females.

The maid ignored them and grabbed Annag's hand, boldly leading her from the yard. "The smithy be on that right corner, do ye see? Two doors down. Will you be safe to go there on your own?"

"Yes, thank you. And if I happen to miss my companion, he is the tall, handsome gentleman with a ginger beard. Hopefully he will not come in and ask for me by name."

"I will try to catch him, my lady. My name is Alice, if you should need more help." She smiled and bobbed a quick curtsy before hurrying back into the inn.

Annag was still shaking as she hurried down the dirty street. Pray

God, she thought, that she had not been seen. All she wanted to do was find James and get out of the little mill town.

She thudded into a hard male chest as she rounded the corner the maid had indicated.

"Oh!" she exclaimed, afraid to look up, knowing it was her fault for hiding her face.

"Anna! Is that you? What is wrong?"

"Oh, James!" She flung herself into his arms. "We must hide!"

He looked down at her with some amusement, then saw that she was serious and his face wrinkled with concern. "Very well. Come with me." He took her hand and walked her behind the blacksmith's building. "You are shaking, my dear. What is wrong? You look as though you have seen a ghost."

"It is far, far worse! Calder's uncle is at the inn. If he sees us together, he will have Tommy taken away from me!"

"Hush, now," he said, drawing her back into his arms.

She was still shaking and began to cry.

"He was at the inn?" he asked, as if to confirm what he had heard.

She nodded into his chest.

"There now, my dear. I have never seen you so upset. We will avoid the inn."

"I was so afraid he would see me, and then I feared you would come inside, looking for me."

"Perhaps it would be for the best if you travelled the rest of the way in a carriage. I can lead your horse.

She shook her head in disapproval. "I do not wish to be alone."

"I understand. I am certain we could hire a maid to accompany you. It is but twenty miles now."

Annag felt alarmed at the thought of this being her final parting from James. She could not do it. "I would rather wait for you. Surely he cannot be making a long stay here?"

He looked at her strangely, but conceded. "I will see if there is somewhere we can wait. Is there anyone at the inn who could inform us when he has gone?"

"The young barmaid. She helped me to escape."

"You really are afraid of him," he remarked, holding her back from him to look into her face. She felt her chin begin to tremble and her teeth chattered.

"I will not let him take Tommy away from you, Anna."

"The situation will be bad enough once they hear about Fenella, as they are sure to do, but if I am also seen to be of loose morals, then they will keep him from me."

"Nothing could be further from the truth, but I know how people would misconstrue our being seen together. I will do everything in my power to protect you, you must know that."

Annag could only hope it would be enough.

CHAPTER 16

*J*ames had had no idea how tormented Anna had been. Suddenly, he felt fiercely protective. He realized he might have to wed her. He had never stopped loving her, of course, but even though they were friends, marriage to him would be very difficult for her. Even if she was willing, he did not want to ask it of her.

She would eventually come to resent him. Their children would not have the same luxuries as her son. However, if her good name was at risk, he would give her his name.

They were now travelling in a carriage for the rest of the journey to London, Anna wrapped in his arms. She had cried herself to sleep. Once he had seen her well hidden in the safekeeping of the blacksmith's wife, he had gone back to the inn and decided a change of transport was for the best. He had arranged for Sancho and Morag to be taken to Waverley's summer estate, which was not far from London. He had considered leaving Sancho there while he was in London anyway. The old fellow deserved a rest. Morag could readily be sent for if Anna needed her, but he thought it would be safer, in terms of travelling incognito, to be within the confines of a carriage.

As far as his heart was concerned, it was aching with the feel of her in his arms.

It was for the best that she had slept all the way to London, he concluded, as the post-chaise pulled in front of Calder House. He had expected it to be a grand mansion similar to Waverley's, but the sight of it underscored the difference in their stations beyond anything else. He did not even keep rooms in London or yet in a house so grand anywhere. Alchnanny would very likely fit within the confines of Calder House with room to spare.

His arm was asleep, but the pain of it awakening was a good reminder that not everything about Anna could be pleasant. He was lying to himself, but anything was better than the truth.

"Anna, my dear, we have arrived."

He watched the phases of awaking on her face—yawning and stretching, then realizing her dishevelment from her crying and ensuing sleep.

It took her a moment, but she realized where she was. "We are in London?"

"At Calder House. I think it would be better if you went in alone. Your bags have already been carried inside."

"But do you not wish to come in and learn if there is any news?"

"I would imagine Waverley knows, but I will call on you first thing in the morning."

He sensed her hesitance. He felt it too. He never wanted to let her go, but the interlude had come to an end—a time he had never thought to have with her again. It would be a precious memory as he grew old alone.

She began to move from the seat, then turned and threw her arms around him. Soon they were kissing with desperation, as though they both knew it was for the last time.

Even through his beard, he could feel her tears.

"Promise me this will not be the end, James."

A knock on the carriage door saved him from answering. "Annag?" came the voice of Laird McKiernan.

She opened the door. "Yes, Father. I had fallen asleep and James was trying to awaken me."

"I am so glad you have arrived. Your mother is hysterical. Is that you, Frome? Will you come in?"

"He thinks it safer if I go in alone. He will call in the morning."

"Thank you for escorting her here safely," McKiernan said and extended his hand. James shook it firmly. "I will call in the morning. I assume Waverley is *au courant* on the matter?"

"Indeed. I do not know where we would be without him."

"Good night, my laird, my lady." James inclined his head and tapped on the roof of the chaise before anything more could be said.

Waverley was just arriving at home with the Duchess, Margo and Lady Innis when James arrived, no doubt looking weary and travel worn. He certainly felt it. They were looking splendid in their evening dress. His sister looked like a princess herself until she realized who the stranger was at the door, whereupon she lost all sense of decorum and threw her arms about him. "James!"

"You look as pretty as a princess, Margo. How are you enjoying your Season? I have heard you are dubbed this Season's diamond."

Her face fell a little. He would have to explore the reason later because he had to greet the Duke and Duchess.

"Frome." Waverley held out a hand for a brotherly shake. James then bowed over Meg's hand.

"Come on inside," she greeted him at once. "I am certain Luke will wish to discuss serious matters with you. Personally, I would enjoy removing my dancing slippers." She led Lady Innis ahead, into the mansion.

"I will come and see you later if you are still awake. If not, we will speak in the morning and you can tell me everything." He kissed his sister's cheek before she followed the Duchess up the wide staircase.

Waverley's butler had already dismissed James' postilion and ordered his bags to be taken inside. That was another thing he would have to deal with later, he thought with an inward groan, but he was too tired to argue at the moment.

The ladies having both retired upstairs, Waverley led him into the study, where a fire was burning to ward off the evening chill. James knew not to stand on ceremony and removed his boots with a sigh of relief, accepting a glass of whisky in Waverley's study.

"You brought some contraband with you, did you?"

"But of course. Why do you think we brought extra carriages to Scotland?" Waverley returned with a naughty grin.

"Tsk." James imitated the sound of disapproval his mother made. "Nevertheless, I am grateful I will not have to drink any French rubbish. How can it be that England has yet to discover how to make anything beyond that abomination blue ruin?"

"Why should we take the bother when others will do it for us?"

"Such a very British sentiment, your Grace. Should that not be the new motto displayed on the country's crest?"

Waverley tossed back the remainder of his glass with another fiendish grin, then refilled the vessel before seating himself across from James.

"You have made good time, even though you were travelling with Lady Calder."

"She was pluck to the backbone about the whole. Well, until we saw one of her son's trustees near Saint Albans, that is, when she feared for her reputation."

"I suspect there is a story there... nasty trustee and heir to the earldom waiting to catch Lady Calder at something with which to declare her an unfit mother and keep her from the son, perchance?"

"A very accurate supposition. If we *were* seen, I will need to marry her and will most likely be begging you for that position within your company before the week is out."

"The offer always stands, as you well know. The company is far better established now than it was a few years ago."

James was still not sure that, as an occupation, it was what he wanted to do, but if it was necessary for Anna, then he would.

"I sent the horses to your summer estate by the way. Necessity dictated that we should disguise ourselves better in a carriage for the last stages of the journey."

"Your ugly beast will be treated like royalty."

"My thanks. *Handsome is as handsome does.* Has there been any word on Lady Fenella? Has any more been discovered thus far? Anna has been beside herself, not having received any news the last few days. Is it certain Bexley is the villain?" The questions fell from James' lips.

Waverley nodded, his expression grave. "He did not reveal his hand until early this morning. The girl has been gone long enough that the *ton* has begun to whisper."

James cursed.

"He is still in London, of course—where better to hide? And he sent everyone on a wild-goose chase lasting several days while he sat back and laughed."

"His tactical mastermind was why he was tolerated, was it not, despite his notorious history with young innocents? I am therefore not surprised he has employed such schemes here."

"We should have disposed of him long ago."

"I had great difficulty explaining to Anna why leadership knew what he was yet looked the other way. It sounded very trite, even to my own ears as I related the tale."

Waverley inclined his head. "The fish will not escape the hook this time. I feel partly responsible. He was under Major Blake's command until he took over himself."

Major Blake was the Duchess's uncle—a blackguard who had kidnapped her and tried to force her into marriage with an American, an equally reprehensible character who sold illegal goods to the French. "You had enough problems in your own regiment. We all knew and did nothing because he was such a good strategist." James felt equal disgust.

Waverley sneered. "A prime example of using evil toward advantage."

"And now Lady Fenella is paying for our looking the other way."

"It is the reason I am determined to ferret him of his hole. I am vexed beyond measure that I have not found him already."

"What contact did he make?"

"Lady Fenella was permitted to send her father a letter."

"Clever. Let me guess, they were going to elope, but something occurred to prevent it, but now she is ruined and needs her dowry?"

"Something along those lines, yes."

"And if he does not receive the dowry first, there can be no wedding?"

"You and I both know he intends no wedding. How can he think to show his face in England, or in the army, after this?"

"He will not. I have already apprised Wellington and the War Office of what has happened. Now that the war is over, there is no one left to stand behind him. However, no one is to apprise him of anything until Lady Fenella is safe in the bosom of her family."

"Where do you think he is hiding her?"

"We are drawing in on Covent Garden or thereabouts—somewhere a man like him can remain anonymous. Now that we know they are in Town, we are closing in a circle around him. Thackeray and Tobin have also arrived. We will meet in the morning to plan our attack. Hopefully, my men will have more information when we meet. It will come as no surprise to you that they tend to find out more information at night and report here first thing."

"Then let us hope they have a fruitful night. My patience has run out where Bexley is concerned."

ANNAG WAS SO weary when they arrived in London that she became tearful again. Her father hugged her warmly and led her into the house, doubtless not understanding that her tears were from fear she would lose James as well as Tommy.

It had been years since she had been to Calder House, and it was as cold and uninviting as before. When she had offered the use of it to her family for the Season, she had been secretly delighted her late husband's equally pompous servants would be forced to wait upon her gauche Scottish family. She had not informed the household she would not be accompanying her parents. Now, however, she felt guilt that she had not been present to prevent the disaster she had predicted. Fenella had not heeded any of her warnings but Annag had been too selfish to want to return to the source of so much pain. Well, now she was here, and the pain was far more acute than before.

Her father led her into the study, a room Calder had never allowed her to enter. He sat her next to the fire, where she felt chilled more from fear than the weather. Her father looked haggard, as though he had aged a decade in a matter of weeks. Poor Papa. She had forgiven him, she realized, as he placed a glass of spirits in her hand then sat next to her. It felt like a peace offering of sorts.

Even though she wished to sit and brood, it was now time to face what she had come to London for. "Have you received any news?"

"We received a note from your sister, the silly chit, just this morning. I had warned your mother about her capriciousness, but I am afraid the blame is equally mine."

"I have been remonstrating with myself in equal measure. I had thought, that even though she is so very silly, she would not ruin herself."

"With being brought up in Scotland, the thought of a Gretna wedding does not perhaps bear quite as much shame as in the south, though she has been told nonetheless."

"No doubt Bexley romanticized the notion," she said tartly. "Then they did elope. I suppose I should be relieved. How, then, came we to miss them? Captain Frome and I looked very thoroughly for any sign of their marriage in Gretna Green. Perhaps they took a different route on the way north."

"You misunderstand me, daughter. Fenella was led to believe Gretna was their destination, but states Bexley had some untimely losses that prevented him having the funds to undertake such a journey or marriage."

Annag's heart fell.

"She has been with this man for two weeks, Annag. The Duke and Duchess have been kind enough to take Innis under their wing and have tried to prevent speculation. But after so long, I am certain people will suspect, even if they do not know. She did not behave sufficiently well to give anyone reason for the benefit of the doubt."

"Do you tell me he refuses to marry her? Did she say where she was? I assume he wants money to hold his tongue."

"That is not how Fenella worded it, of course—she still has delusions of becoming Mrs. Bexley—but I can read between the lines well enough. Why would he have her when he can just have the money?"

"That is what we suspected," Annag agreed.

"What I cannot understand, daughter, is why the Duke has taken this matter upon himself. We are severely indebted to him in ways you are, most likely, unaware of. I did not know where to begin, other than to hope they had merely eloped and we would attempt to salvage the situation later. But even a duke and duchess cannot repair Fenella's good name once this becomes known."

"I believe the Duke and Captain Frome feel it to be their duty to bring Bexley to heel—something to do with serving with him in the army. Captain Frome intimated this was not the first time Bexley had ruined a young lady, but he was tolerated because of his excellence with military strategy."

"It would not be the first time," her father said cynically.

"Do you intend to pay him the money? I assume the request was exorbitant?"

"Three times the amount of her dowry. Yet what else can I do?"

"Do nothing until you have consulted with the Duke and the Captain. I suspect they are determining a plan at this very moment. Allow them to help before paying him as much as a penny."

"How long will he be patient? I would wager he has only waited this long to make certain we had little other choice." He stood and refilled his glass.

"There is no way in which he might be persuaded to marry her? I know it is less than ideal, but would at least save her reputation."

"As if he cares anything for that," her father growled. "No, I could not wish for such a thing even for her sake. Her mother and I merely want her home safely. Perhaps we may find someone in Scotland who will have her."

"I am confident that whatever plan the Duke and Captain come up with will be for the best, Papa."

"I am quite prepared to do whatever they wish. How could I presume otherwise? I still cannot fathom their willingness to help. They are two remarkable young men. I fully admit I have quite underestimated young Frome. Would that I could go back and change events for you, Annag. Calder made you very unhappy, did he not?"

"There is no good to be had in dredging up such things now. You did what you thought was best at the time."

"I do not think I am worthy of such credit. I will admit I did not think Frome a good match, but I should not have forced him to go away. Will you forgive me?"

"You are already forgiven. As a mother, I now find it easier to understand your actions." James had been forced to leave? Somehow it had been easier to think that he had gone of his own volition—not that it changed anything now.

"Nonetheless, I owe you an apology, as I do the Captain. I am indebted to him, as well, for escorting you here safely and for assisting in the search for your sister. It is his connection to Waverley that has brought us any hope."

"Let us pray we may find her safely. From what I hear of Bexley, he is ruthless." She finished her small amount of spirits, and feeling warm and sleepy, rose. "Forgive me, Papa, but I must seek my bed. We have spent several long, hard days in the saddle, and endured not the most comfortable nights at a dozen crowded inns."

"I am glad you are here. You will be a great source of comfort to your mother."

Annag climbed the stairs to her old apartment, trying not to think about where she was or what had happened there. As she slipped from her dusty, worn riding habit, which she hoped never to see again, she went through the motions of washing herself with the warm water that someone had at least been thoughtful enough to provide. She was too tired to order a bath. She brushed out her hair, trying not to let demons of the past and present creep into her thoughts. It was always so at night, in the darkness with no light to fend them off. She could not help but think of her dear Tommy and how she would send him a letter in the morning. It was almost time for his school holiday, but at least she was nearby. If she had to bring him to London, then she would. This was his house, after all.

She looked around at the opulent room, where deep rose curtains and matching bed hangings accentuated green and gold wallpaper dotted with delicate roses. If only James could understand how little she needed any of this. How could she make him understand? Her time in Scotland had been the happiest of her life. The only way it could have been better was if she could have shared it with Tommy.

She climbed into the large bed and, being honest with herself, did appreciate the comfort in that, at least. Yet she would give up even a soft mattress to be with James—to be happy.

But first, they had to find Fenella and try to minimize the scandal. She was afraid the price of doing so would be very, very high.

The lure of sleep finally captured her as she thought of James and Tommy riding, running and laughing together in the meadow at Alchnanny that they loved so much. She hoped it would one day be more than just a dream.

CHAPTER 17

*J*ames shot up in his bed and looked around to gather his bearings. It was just like being in the army. He was alert with every little noise, but likewise could sleep anywhere. *Waverley Place, London.* He was there to look for Lady Fenella. The brethren had gathered there.

"Good morning, sir," the servant said as he drew the curtains. James saw that a fresh bowl of steaming water awaited him. "Would you care for a fire?"

In the summer? It felt like Hades in the capital compared with Scotland. "No, thank you."

"I have been sent to help you dress. The other gentlemen will breakfast in half an hour, his Grace asked me to inform you."

"As you can see, I will not be needing a shave." He almost got a smile out of the servant, but he was too well trained. "I will dress myself."

A bath had been waiting for him when he had finally finished talking to Waverley the evening before. He would do well not to become accustomed to search luxuries, he told himself firmly.

"Very good, sir. If you require anything, please ring."

James forced his tired limbs from the bed and went over to splash his face and wet his hair before running a comb through his untamed locks and beard. He noticed his clothing had been cleaned, pressed and laid out for him, and his boots shined, looking newer than the day he purchased them. That was stretching actuality, of course, but he had never thought to see them looking so fine again.

Once dressed, he made his way to the breakfast room, where the Duke was already holding court. James could not repress his smile. Some things never changed. He was happy to see his friends again, even if it was for a less than ideal purpose.

"Top o' the mornin' to you," a deep Irish brogue called from beside him.

"Tobin! Sneaking up on a fellow as usual, you old rogue!"

"Aye, of course!" Tobin set down his plate, then hugged James as equally hard as he himself was squeezing back.

Thackeray came limping in and joined in the mêlée of greetings and embraces. No one in the *ton* would believe their eyes if they saw this group of gentlemen behaving like young boys.

It was some minutes before they actually sat down with plates of food to eat. James realized how much he missed—no, needed—this fellowship. It was something he needed to consider, but now was not the time.

"Has anyone heard from Philip? It seems wrong not to have him here. This is his area of expertise," Thackeray remarked.

"Did someone speak of the devil?" Philip asked from the doorway. He was bronzed from the sun, his hair was too long, and he made every other man pale in comparison.

"How do you do that?" James asked, waving his hand. "Appear as though conjured, looking like a Greek god."

Philip flashed him a smile before coming into the room to greet them one by one.

"I thought you were to be gone at least another month," Waverley added with a frown. James knew it was not because the Duke did not wish for his presence, but because, in his orderly existence, he needed to know everything.

"My man happened to send your letter just as we were considering returning home. Amelia is in the family way again, and this was a good excuse to return. She will never be the first to admit defeat."

All of them laughed. It was so very true. Amelia was as game a female as ever lived. She liked to be in the middle of anything resembling action. Tobin, Philip and James had worked on an operation with her, which had resulted in Philip becoming leg-shackled.

"I have little doubt she will be here just as soon as the nausea she is subject to each morning has passed for today."

"Well, your timing is perfect," Waverley acknowledged.

Philip filled his plate from the array of dishes on the sideboard and joined them at the table.

"It is good of you all to come," the Duke said courteously.

"We would all come, at any time you called," Tobin remarked, "but I think each one of us knows what Bexley is capable of, and feel a measure of responsibility that he is still in a position to commit such atrocities." They all murmured their agreement, but James knew it was very personal for Tobin.

Before Tobin had become the Duke's batman, he had been under Major Harrison's and then Captain Bexley's command, and had suffered unnameable punishments at their hands when first enlisted. He knew more than most what they were capable of.

"My men believe they have Bexley's location, narrowed down, so I think the best course will be to unearth and confront him as soon as possible. Tonight."

"Having invested a great deal of time into the scheme of Lady Fenella, Bexley ain't about to go quietly without his money," Tobin warned.

"Do you think he suspects we are searching?" Philip asked.

"I cannot be certain," answered Waverley, "but it is likely he has heard that Lady Fenella's sister is being chaperoned by the Duchess."

"In that case, he will see it as more than a conquest of Lady Fenella. He will want to best the brethren. It is all a game to him." Phillip contemplated.

"Indeed, but we will not allow that to happen," the Duke said with a low growl that James had not heard since their days on the Peninsula.

"What is the plan thus far?" Philip asked, shedding his charming mien and reverting immediately to that of lethal spy. Although James had worked closely with Philip, he had never quite mastered the same dangerous demeanour.

"Surround him. Of course, it is not as simple as that. I expect details to be delivered to Laird McKiernan this morning as to how we are to provide the funds Bexley requires for his silence."

"I expect a well-contrived scheme on Bexley's part. It will not be a simple matter of, 'Leave a bank draft for me at my club,'" Tobin said, mimicking the villain in a high voice.

"If I were he, I would somehow use Fenella as bait," James remarked.

"I agree," Tobin said. "He will make the exchange very public though, somewhere like Hyde Park during the fashionable hour. Where better to run and hide than amongst a large crowd?"

"And, dare I say, if he strolls the paths on with Lady Fenella on his arm, everyone will see them together, underlying the threat, if McKiernan does not comply," Philip added.

"I think you are correct," Waverley said, gesturing towards his former batman and clearly thinking over Tobin's assessment. "It is the perfect setting for events to work in Bexley's favour."

"We will need dozens of men to capture him there," Philip said.

Thackeray, who had always been the deepest thinker, the one who only spoke when he had something relevant to say, tapped the table. "You need the element of surprise."

"How do you mean, beyond the obvious?" James asked, knowing Thackeray would have already thought of it.

"Ladies," came the succinct reply.

They all knew what he meant, which was why no one spoke immediately.

"Well, I know my wife would be the first to volunteer, but I cannot say I want her involved whilst in her present condition," Philip said quietly.

"Do you not think it wrong for us to ask ladies to fight our battles when they have not been trained in such concerns?" Waverley objected.

"Indeed, with the exception of her Grace, Amelia is perhaps the only one who will realize what we might be dealing with," Philip agreed.

"My Duchess will not be involved in this," Waverley growled again.

"You know as well as I how clever Bexley is," Thackeray answered. "He will be expecting one of us."

"Then one of us he shall get." The Duke slammed his fist on the table.

"I was not suggesting they be left unprotected," Thackeray protested, "only that we take him off guard by presenting him with one—or two—of them instead of one of us or Laird McKiernan."

"That could serve, you know." Tobin spoke up after brooding on the matter in silence.

James knew the obvious answer, but he could not like putting Anna in such a position. "Can we not think of any other way?" he asked.

"I believe the only other way depends on the number of men you can call upon. We surround him on all sides."

"But that is what he will be expecting. He will have a means of escape," Tobin argued.

"What I do not understand is why would he be willing to commit immolation in such a public manner? He has to know he will be exiled, at the very least." Philip shook his head. "It does not seem at all like Bexley."

"Perhaps he did not realize Lady Fenella's connection to us until it was too late," James suggested. "She would have seemed easy prey to him, at first glance—the daughter of a minor Scottish peer, with a sizeable dowry but no real connections in Society."

"It fits," Thackeray agreed.

"So he will be desperate and the risk is very high," Philip surmised.

"Would one of her sisters be willing to help?" Tobin asked at the same moment as a knock sounded on the door. Waverley stared at the offending panel as though whoever was behind it should be petrified to a pillar of stone for disturbing them. After a moment, he decided it must be important. "Enter," he called.

"Lady Calder, your Grace."

All the brethren stood as Anna entered the room, looking pale. James immediately went to her. "What has happened?"

Anna held out a folded note. "It seems the time has come."

James took the letter and opened it.

5 PM ON ROTTEN ROW. Your daughter and her reputation in exchange for 15,000 pounds.

"IT IS UNSIGNED, OF COURSE." James could not help but look at Tobin first. "It seems you have his measure, old fellow."

"Lady Calder, would you be willing to help us catch Bexley?" Thackeray asked.

James wanted to reach across and strangle Matthias.

"Of course. I will do anything," she answered.

"LET us remove to the drawing room where we may discuss this more comfortably," the Duke said.

Annag had been on her way to visit Innis when an urchin had delivered the note. She had convinced her father to allow her to deliver it. He was still trying to determine how to gather the funds in such a short time.

James led her by the arm into the other room. He had not let her go since she had arrived, and she was quite content for him to continue to hold her. She had not stopped shaking since reading the note. It was all far more threatening and real, now that she had seen it. Fenella was nothing but a commodity to be disposed of at Bexley's whim.

"Please take a seat. Tea, Timmons, and perhaps something stronger," the Duke said, indicating to his butler to see to the task.

"You gentlemen, then, are the infamous brethren," Annag remarked after the introductions had been made and she was sitting in a circle with James, his Grace of Waverley, Lords Thackeray and Lord Kilmorgan, and Captain Elliott. "I cannot tell you how grateful I am for your assistance. My father and I still do not quite understand why you would go to such lengths to help us, but we are most grateful nevertheless."

Waverley spoke. "This is our battle to fight, my lady. We are pleased to lend you our assistance."

"I regret the manner of our meeting, gentlemen," she acknowledged them politely, "yet cannot but be thankful you should consider the matter of personal importance. How may I be of help?"

"As you and I have already discussed, Bexley is first-rate at scheming," James began. "By now, he will have realized that your sister is under our protection, although later than we would have wished."

"There are many wrongs we should have righted long ago," one of the men said, his tone held a hint of an Irish lilt. She was not certain she could remember who was whom.

"We were just discussing that we might be able to surprise Bexley by using ladies to distract him," James explained.

"It was merely a suggestion, and one I cannot like," the Duke interjected.

"I think it only fair that I be involved," Annag remarked. "It seems you all have a grievance with him from the past, but I do as well. This concerns my sister, and I was not here to protect her. What would you suggest? He has certainly chosen his rendezvous well. It not only gives him a very public place with innumerable escape routes, it also puts my sister on display in front of the entire *ton*. Should someone dare to thwart him, then it is easy for him to ruin her with a few simple, well-chosen words—or actions."

"We have not planned the details yet. Someone has to meet them. He will be expecting your father."

171

"I see. He will be quite shocked to have me instead, will he not?" Annag said with a small smile. "What will happen then?"

"That is what we must decide. If you do not take the money to him, then he will shout to the world that Lady Fenella has been in his sole company these past two weeks."

"Is it possible Lady Calder could take enough funds to fob him off? Or take a sack with sham money beneath the real? I confess it would please me greatly to hoodwink him," the Irishman remarked.

"I suspect he would then be out for revenge, or would at the very least escape without repercussion. I cannot like it," the Duke said. "It would be better to finish this now."

"What about a diversion?" the dark, handsome one asked. Elliott?

"It might work if it were safeguarded against accident or interference. We would have to make certain he had no opportunity to make an audience of those members of the *ton* present. It takes only one person to hear and gossip," James countered.

"That would necessitate surrounding him with the army." The blond, quiet one finally spoke.

"That might not be a bad idea, but we have little time to set the trap," the Duke said. Annag could all but see his mind working.

"He will have done that a-purpose," the Irishman sneered with obvious loathing.

"Do you think he will be in uniform to draw attention? Because if you surround him with militia, most will be ranked well below him, and fear retribution or charges of insubordination," James pointed out.

"An excellent point, but if they have been given specific orders as to him being apprehended for court martial, I think they would obey an officer ranked above a major," the Duke said, but he was used to being obeyed without question. Annag now understood what James had meant earlier.

"If anyone can achieve that level of obedience, it would be you, your Grace. I think it is our best plan on little notice. Lady Calder will meet Bexley and her sister, and mayhap arrange for some type of military review at the same time."

"Then how do we draw them over to Rotten Row? Military reviews are held on the Parade Ground."

The men were talking back and forth so quickly, Annag could scarcely follow who was saying what.

"I do not want Lady Calder to meet them alone," James declared flatly. "Bexley could easily draw her in. I assure you, he will be armed."

"There is strength in numbers," Waverley conceded.

As he spoke, the Duchess entered with Innis and Margo, but stopped short at the sight of the group. "I do beg your pardon, but Timmons told me Lady Calder was here. I assumed she had called to visit her sister." She looked from one to the other of the grave faces. "You have had news." It was not a question.

The Duke nodded and led the Duchess to a seat. Innis was already rushing towards Annag, and Margo had sought James' side.

"All things considered, it is probably best to inform you all of the plan. We may need your help. Much though I cannot like it, the idea has merit if you are willing."

The idea was repeated to the other three ladies. Without hesitation, they all agreed to help. It was decided that the group of them would meet Bexley and Lady Fenella in the park. Waverley would try to enlist the support of one of the Guards' regiments to surround the ladies, and hopefully protect them as they made the transaction, while the brethren would be strategically placed about the perimeter near the gates.

"Amelia will not want to miss the trick. She will never forgive me."

"Kitty will want to take part as well," the blond gentleman said. "After all, it was my suggestion to employ the ladies. It seems only fair."

"Wal, now, in that case, might I be offering Bridget's services as well?" the Irishman cut in sardonically.

"I believe I should go and speak with the War Office. One of you organize the ladies and one of you decide where we should position ourselves in the Park," the Duke said to the gentlemen. "Meet here again at three for final plans. I would like to be in place by four of the clock."

Everyone voiced their agreement.

"Would anyone care to accompany me?"

The dark, handsome one agreed to go, and the two of them left without further ado.

"I would like to go and survey the Park," the Irishman said.

"I will join you. I may not be able to sit a horse as well as I used to, but my eyes still work well." The blond man limped to his feet and made the ladies an elegant bow.

"It looks as though you are left with my sparkling conversation for your entertainment," James teased the ladies when the other gentlemen had gone.

"I think we should send for Amelia. She really is the best suited to such intrigue," the Duchess remarked with a fond smile.

James leaned over to whisper in Annag's ear. "Another redhead," he explained.

"Ah."

The Duchess rang for more tea and cakes to be brought it in while they waited for Amelia to join them. Annag asked how Margo and Innis were enjoying London, and they were suitably subdued by the events surrounding Fenella.

"We have tried our best to pretend as though nothing is wrong, but I fear treading the boards at Drury Lane will never be my calling," Innis said.

"Thank God for that," Annag drawled.

"It is hard to trust anyone after what Major Bexley has done. He was so charming, Annag!" she exclaimed, as though she still could not believe him to be a villain.

"They usually are," she agreed. "And you, Miss Frome? How do you like London?"

"It is all so overwhelming and beautiful. I am glad for the experience."

Annag sensed hesitation. "There is something amiss?"

"I will be glad to return home, my lady. I think I am better suited to the country," she added with a blush.

Annag could not help but look at James, who understood very well what his sister meant. She hoped he would allow the match.

It did not seem long at all before a striking woman swept into the room, making it feel small. Next to the Duchess, it was hard to imagine two more beautiful women. The new arrival's hair was the most glorious mane of red that Annag had ever seen, and she had seen an abundance.

"Allow me to present my sister, Lady Amelia Elliott," the Duchess of Waverley said.

James had risen to bow over her hand.

"I hear we have another operation to perform together, Captain Frome. It will be quite like old times," Lady Amelia said with an impish gleam in her eye.

"Let us hope this operation is a good deal simpler," James said, with an obvious familiarity that made Annag jealous.

CHAPTER 18

*J*ames spent the next couple of hours trying to prepare the ladies for all possible eventualities.

"We are far more capable than you think, James," Lady Amelia said. "It is part of our education as ladies to notice everything about gentlemen."

He laughed. "On reflection, I should prefer not to know, but I believe you. I mean no insult; we want only for you to be safe. Bexley is ruthless and accustomed to killing. He will not think twice about sacrificing one of you to save himself. However, by being in the middle of Hyde Park, he will put himself at a disadvantage, as he will discover when he is surrounded by ladies. It is a wise move to use you, strategically speaking, I can but hope it will give him pause. Even he knows he cannot easily harm one of you without severe repercussions."

"I am feeling rather merciless," Anna said, "knowing what he has done to my sister…" The ladies murmured their agreement. "…and to all the other young innocents he has harmed,"

"I do not intend that he shall ever be able to hurt another person when we have done with him," Lady Amelia added.

James was surprised by how ruthless the ladies seemed when one of their own sex had been compromised. Had he known, he would have been far more afraid of them when he was younger. Bexley's chances, he mused maliciously, were much slimmer with this group of Furies against him.

Once satisfied with their plan, he left with Anna to visit Laird McKiernan. He wanted to ensure that Bexley would not be able to tell he was being duped.

However, McKiernan was less easy to convince of the expediency of allowing Anna to make the exchange. After James had taken the time to explain their strategy, and given him another position in which to feel useful, however, his lairdship grudgingly gave his consent. He had also made James a very unexpected apology for his actions against James ten years prior. It did not erase his sins, but it did help to hear it somehow.

By the time James returned to Waverley Place, a large luncheon had been set out in the dining room, and most of the party was eating and chatting nervously in anticipation of what was to come.

Waverley and Philip were the last to arrive.

"Did you meet with success?" James asked.

"Yes, after promising my second-born and several votes. There will not be a review, but instead a company of Guards will arrive at the appointed time on their way to drill in the park."

"Do you think Bexley will credit that?" Tobin asked.

"I am hoping he will be too preoccupied to notice precisely why the cavalry is there. We have support, and that is all that matters."

"As long as they are there and know what is expected."

"Are the ladies prepared?" Waverley asked. "I am still concerned about the wisdom of asking them to put themselves at risk."

"I think it only fitting that our wives be involved. They are part of the brethren now," Philip said, looking fondly at his wife.

James did not mention that not all of them were wives. It seemed unnecessary but he thought it nonetheless as he looked over at Anna with pride. She had remained calm and poised through this whole business, and she had the biggest part to play. He walked over to her. "Are you certain you wish to do this?"

She looked up at him with determination. "Of course. I consider this situation to be my responsibility. Nevertheless, I hope he will relinquish Fenella before insisting upon counting every note."

"If he is so charitable as to let her go, then take her and back away as quickly as possible. The Guards will surround him as soon as you are clear."

She nodded. They had repeated the plan many times.

"You have your pistol in your pocket, in case it should prove necessary?" he asked, even though he knew she did. They had already practised how to shoot it that afternoon.

"I do not think there is anything else to do. I shall be happy when this afternoon is over."

"I always felt the same way before a battle. The waiting was worse than the action."

"James," Anna said, pulling him away from the others. "I wish I had time to thank you properly. I believe you know how I feel about you, but I wanted to say it, nevertheless."

"Do not speak as though this is the end." He tried to reassure her and himself at the same time. He had chosen a position where he hoped to have a clean shot at Bexley were it to become necessary, although when one was mounted nothing was guaranteed. James did not want Anna to declare her love and say words of goodbye, but still he pulled her close and kissed the top of her head, hoping she would understand.

When the time came, the ladies divided into two carriages to arrive separately, and the men rode on horseback. James would not be surprised in the least if Bexley had people watching Calder House and Waverley Place. With that in mind, the brethren did not leave together or by the front door.

It was a warm summer's day and there were already a lot of people milling about, even though it was not quite the fashionable hour. James hoped that the children flying kites and laughing and chasing the geese would not be subjected to a display of violence.

"Assume you are being watched, gentlemen," Waverley reminded them as they parted to go to their respective positions. Rotten Row stretched the length of the Park and Bexley could, of course, mean anywhere along the path, but the brethren suspected he would choose the more crowded end, where the promenade took place. If he chose to bring Lady Fenella on horseback, the whole operation would become much more difficult. That is why they had decided to remain on their mounts so they could give chase.

Anna would be with Lady Innis and his sister, Margo, holding the reticule of bank notes and paper. They would be drawn up and engaged in conversation with the Duchess, Lady Thackeray and Lady Kilmorgan in the second carriage. Lady Amelia had insisted on keeping watch on the perimeter, as Philip had expressly forbidden her from riding after Bexley.

They had cleverly fashioned stacks of paper with real notes on the ends of each bundle so, even if Bexley succeeded in taking the money, there would be far less than he expected.

James had asked to be closest to the ladies in order to protect Anna, and the Duke had reluctantly conceded. The other ladies should not be in too much danger, he believed, since they would be in a carriage… as long as bullets did not fly. James knew the brethren would not be careless with their aim, and the cavalry was there to help prevent Bexley from escaping, but not to shoot, yet plans had been known to go wrong…

James took his position behind some trees until there were enough vehicles and other riders for him to safely blend in behind. The other brethren were doing the same, though occasionally he would spot one of them amongst the crowd, keen eyes scanning for their target.

At five o'clock sharp, James saw the Duchess's open landau come into view with her Grace looking for all the world as though she were holding court on any normal day. Society had always been fascinated by her angelic beauty and graciousness. Whenever she made an appearance, all eyes were drawn to her as they were now. It was a few more minutes before James saw Anna, Innis and Margo pull up along-side the Waverley carriage as they had planned, greeting each other as though it had been weeks instead of minutes since they had last seen one another.

If the ladies were nervous, they were doing an excellent job of hiding it. James continued to scan the crowd for any sign of Bexley, fully expecting some trick.

Minutes passed, and the crowd grew to a crush. Carriages were at a standstill.

It was the perfect place for the rendezvous. It was tactical genius and a nightmarish situation in which to defend the leading players.

James checked his pocket watch; it was already fifteen minutes past five. Was Bexley waiting to show himself? It would not surprise James at all. Perhaps he was looking for Laird McKiernan and did not recognize Anna? But Fenella would, unless he had not brought her. It was just like Bexley to make them wait and anticipate events.

Anna looked around, scanning the crowd, probably wondering the same as he. The note had not specified that Laird McKiernan must bring the money himself.

Lady Amelia passed directly in front of him without so much as a flicker of acknowledgement. It had been agreed upon that if there were messages to relay, she would be the one to do it as to minimize suspicion. He watched as she rode up to the carriages and greeted the ladies. James had to admit that they were very, very good at this.

Where were the Guards, he wondered. Perhaps, he mused, Waverley had arranged a signal with them so as not to scare Bexley away.

His horse shuffled impatiently as he stopped to scan for newcomers. James kept the curse under his breath. Would that he had Sancho, who knew better but was also trained to such situations. Minutes felt like hours and drew the intensity and anticipation to a fever pitch.

When the hairs on the back of James' neck tingled, he knew Bexley was nearby, watching. How would the villain show himself?

He turned to watch Anna, but she was no longer in the carriage! What had he missed? It had been only seconds while his gaze had been on the masses of people.

He manoeuvred closer, to be within range, and saw her walking alone, looking like fox bait.

Why had she altered the plan? Was that the message Amelia had passed on to her?

James' heart began to pound, and he felt fear as never before as he urged his mount forward.

~

ANNAG HAD NEVER BEEN SO scared in her life, but she was determined. While James had been away with her father during the afternoon, the ladies had made their own plan. If it appeared as though Bexley would not show himself, then Lady Amelia was to ride by and greet them, signalling for Annag to leave the carriage on her own, thus encouraging Bexley to approach her.

They knew the men would be angry, but sometimes they did not always know what was best. Annag walked around between groups of people conversing, willing her legs to stop shaking, while trying all the while to appear as though she were enjoying the weather and the promenade.

Instead, she could feel the gun in her pocket, and the money in her reticule, weighing her down like cannonballs. She felt conspicuous, as though she had a bright red target painted upon herself.

Would it work? She could not stand there for long, or people might begin to notice the oddity and approach, feeling sorry for her.

Would Bexley be very angry that her father was not waiting for him? She thought he might, if only because his plans were not going exactly as he had ordered.

Annag could hear bells chiming the half-hour somewhere in the distance. She was about to turn back to the carriage when she heard a voice from behind her.

"Turn around and greet me like an old acquaintance," a gravelly voice commanded. "Then you can explain why your father has not come."

Annag turned and forced herself to smile. She held out the hand to him that was not on the gun, allowing him to bow over it. He looked up at her, assessing her as she was assessing him.

"Charmed, Lady Calder." He knew who she was, then. He flashed a smile at her and was indeed extremely handsome with golden hair and dark grey eyes. She could see why someone as young and naïve as Fenella would be enchanted. For herself, she could see the devil behind those dark eyes and practised smile.

"My father had a heart seizure this morning from the anxiety of having to gather 15,000 pounds, sir."

"You are here in his stead?"

"Indeed, but as I do not see my sister, it appears we are at an impasse."

"Do you have the money?"

"Do you have my sister?" she countered in a voice that she prayed sounded more assertive than she felt.

"You will be receiving instructions on how to find your sister when I am assured the money is all there."

"That is not what the note said. I will give you the money when I can see my sister." She glared, trying not to panic. She saw James ride by in her periphery, which should have been reassuring, but she was terrified Bexley would also see him. He knew her name, so he must know of their connection.

Something caught Bexley's gaze and she sensed the change in his demeanour immediately. Annag looked up for an instant and noticed the detachment of mounted Guards. Unfortunately, in that moment, Bexley grabbed her arm, on which hung the reticule of money, and pulled her close, discreetly twisting her arm behind her until she thought it might snap in two. He spoke in her ear. "The money is here, I presume?" He pulled on the bag.

She nodded.

"I suggest you let it go, or I will push you in front of one of those horses. Do you understand?"

"What about my sister, sir?" She was furious, and she also wanted to delay long enough to ensure there was time for the Guards to surround them.

"When I am satisfied all of the money is there, I will send her to you."

"I knew you would not keep your word."

"Oh, but you knew I was not a gentleman or I would have wed your sister. In truth, this is the hardest I have ever had to work for such a paltry sum. I will be relieved to be rid of the brat!"

Annag shoved her elbow into his stomach, causing her to wince with pain. She would suffer later, but it was worth it, even if it did no real harm to him. He wrenched her elbow upwards and having sliced the reticule from her arm, threw her to the ground. As he turned to run away, she managed to hook her boot under his, causing him to stumble. To her fury, the weasel somehow kept his footing, and remained upright and began to run. People had seen her fall and hastened to her aid, forming a circle around her.

Annag had done all she could; the rest would be up to the other brethren.

She saw James heading towards her, but she quickly shook her head and indicated with her head for him to follow. It was likely she had broken her arm, but that could wait.

She smiled at the gentleman who assisted her to her feet. "Thank you for your kindness. I am afraid I am very clumsy. My carriage is just over there, if you would be so kind."

"Annag!" Innis exclaimed, as the cheerful, portly gentleman, who was all solicitousness, helped her to climb into the carriage. She thanked him and waited for him to depart before she turned to her sister.

"Did you see where Bexley went?"

Innis shook her head. "What about you? Did he hurt you?"

"Never mind me, he cannot be allowed to get away!" She scarcely noticed the pain in her arm. All she could think of was where had Bexley gone and would they be able to capture him.

"I saw Amelia chase after him. The Guards had also formed a circle about you," the Duchess said, reaching across to reassure her with her hand. Annag winced.

"You are hurt!" the Duchess exclaimed.

"It is nothing. We must capture Bexley! He would not tell me where Fenella is."

"The gentlemen know him well. They will find him."

Annag scanned the crowd with a sense of desperation, and she saw the Guards' large hats some distance from the crowd, but they did not appear to be moving.

"Over there! Driver!"

"Perhaps it is better if we stay here," one of the ladies said. "The gentlemen will follow Bexley."

Annag knew that was the rational thing to do, but she was beyond such reasoning. "You stay here, I must go. Innis, Margo, if you do not wish to follow, climb into the other carriage. Quickly!"

Both girls shook their heads. "I will stay with you," Innis said. "I shall as well," Margo seconded.

"Please follow the guardsmen," Annag said to her driver.

It was not such an easy command to comply with. The crowd seemed to be alerted to the mischief. Had they realized the cavalry was not simply there to practice? They had hoped not to draw attention, but at least Fenella was not there to be shunned in person. If they could find her soon, there might yet be hope.

Unfortunately, the driver could not advance more than a few feet before they were stuck. Annag descended the carriage and began to race towards the circle of guardsmen. Perhaps they would not have let her through if the Duke had not seen her and allowed her to pass. She was not expecting the scene before her when she reached the centre. Bexley was surrounded like a fox caught by hounds. He was face down on the ground, Lady Amelia with her booted heel in his back, and her pistol aimed at his head, and the brethren grouped around her with weapons drawn.

Annag stopped short for a moment, ensuring the situation was safe. Instinctively, she put her hand on her pistol in her pocket and moved closer.

"Stay back, Anna." Her mind registered that James was speaking, but she could not obey. Neither could she allow Lady Amelia to risk herself further. She took a step closer, but someone stayed her with their hand. "Allow us to deal with him, my lady," Lord Kilmorgan said. "You do not want to draw attention to your sister at this moment."

He was right. Annag stepped back.

An officer dismounted from his horse and walked towards Bexley. "Thank you for your assistance, my lady. We will deal with him from here."

"I will release him when he has been bound," Lady Amelia answered curtly.

The colonel looked surprised, but gave the order when Waverley nodded his head.

Annag could not but admire Lady Amelia's pluck.

"He is to be taken by the soldiers?" Annag asked in a whisper.

"Do not worry, it is all for show in case someone is watching. This way, Bexley cannot escape from a superior officer, and to Society it appears to be an army matter. It is, in a way, but were he to begin shouting about your sister, it would only make him look more ridiculous."

"If he begins shouting about my sister, I will not restrain myself."

Lord Kilmorgan smiled down at her, looking every inch a rogue.

Annag was to have no such opportunity. Bexley's arms were bound behind his back, then he was pulled to his feet. His face was curled into a disdainful sneer, and he opened his mouth to speak, but James stepped forward and summarily drew his cork, with a punch square in the nose, preventing whatever he was about to say.

James said something to Bexley that Annag could not hear before he was ushered into a closed carriage that was drawn up nearby, and driven away.

The Guards followed, then the crowd began to disperse, no doubt discussing what had just happened. James walked back to her and handed her the ruined reticule.

Annag looked up at James with tears in her eyes. She wished she could run into his arms, but there were too many people still about.

The other ladies were nearby, spreading the tale they had rehearsed about Bexley. A moment later, James came to her and led her towards her carriage.

"We still do not know where Fenella is," she said softly.

185

"Leave that to us. We have a little experience in drawing secrets from people."

"You were a spy?" she asked with awe.

"I was many things, my lady. Now, return home, if you will. I shall send word as soon as we know something."

He took hold of her arm to hand her into the carriage, and she screamed with pain.

"He hurt you!" James growled. "He will be fortunate, indeed, to live through this day."

"James, pray do not hurt him until you know where my sister is. Now go. I will send for the doctor as soon as I reach Calder House."

He hesitated, but nodded and hurried away. It was not a satisfactory ending to the story yet, but at least they had Bexley.

CHAPTER 19

$\mathcal{U}$nfortunately, Fenella was Bexley's key to keeping his head from swinging and he knew it.

After James had knocked him out, it had taken Bexley a little while to come to his senses. He then became insufferably obstinate as each of the brethren took turns at questioning him in a small, bare room at the Horse Guards. Unfortunately, part of their military training was to withhold information upon questioning, and Bexley knew all the tricks.

He remained silent, speaking only with his eyes. The eyes made it very clear he would not speak to James, so he remained in the background, and allowed the others to apply their skills. Philip was very, very skilled. Tobin went first, mostly taking the time to let Bexley know precisely what he thought about him. No one could throw an insult like a scorned Irishman. Then, the Duke tried to bargain with him, telling him that perhaps he would be allowed to live if he cooperated. Bexley remained unmoved.

Next, Matthias tried a more diplomatic approach, and endeavoured to convince Bexley to be honourable. James knew it would not work, but the more they prolonged the interrogation, the more likely

Bexley would be to submit, although James had seen some prisoners hold out for weeks.

Philip was last, and James sat back and prepared to watch the master.

If anyone could coax Fenella's whereabouts from Bexley, it was he.

Philip sat directly across from the captive. "Shall I go to the bother of wasting my talents on you?" Philip asked while examining his nails.

"I have heard of your reputed skill." Bexley spoke at last. "I was waiting for someone approaching worthy," he sneered.

"What shall it be, then?"

"I will have the funds and be released to spend them on the Continent."

"Never to return to England's shores?" Philip asked. "That hardly seems like a punishment to me."

"You will never be graced with my presence again," the rogue offered superciliously.

"I find that is hardly an incentive either," Philip drawled.

"Prinny will never agree to it," the Duke interrupted. "I might be able to convince him to send you to Australia."

Bexley scoffed, then lounged back in the chair as though he had not a care in the world.

There was a light knock on the door and Waverley exited the room, but Bexley did not move his eyes from Philip.

James wondered what would motivate Bexley. Clearly a man such as he thought he was above rules of proper conduct. Honour did not apply. Beyond money and freedom, would he care about anything?

"If I do not return tonight, my man has instructions on how to deal with Lady Fenella," he drawled insolently. Was he bluffing?

Philip remained quiet, waiting for Bexley to elaborate. James thought Bexley would be tapping his fingers on the table in boredom, were his hands not bound. James suspected Bexley was enjoying this charade.

"However, if you do not care for her reputation, then do with me as you will. She has been absent long enough. People are already talking."

Philip had a way of staring that was most disconcerting. It was absolutely impossible to read his thoughts or know what he would do next.

"We will find her eventually," Philip said calmly, shoving his chair back and quickly standing. "I am inclined to let him starve and soil himself."

Philip walked to the door and the rest of them followed. James was surprised Philip had given up so quickly, but he knew there must be a reason, if only to make Bexley wait.

"Do you think he is bluffing?" Tobin asked, once they were out of earshot of the holding room.

"I have no doubt he has made alternate plans for Lady Fenella, but he wants to toy with us. He thinks he can best us by this game. He is in no way close to talking, so I will not waste my breath."

"What do you propose?" Matthias asked.

"That we return to the Park to see if anyone saw her there with him. Did he intend to exchange her, but then saw us or Lady Calder and changed his mind? I cannot read him well enough to know." Philip shook his head as though it was an inexcusable fault.

"That is an excellent idea. Perhaps he even left her somewhere nearby, though I do not think we were wrong about him coming alone to the rendezvous."

"I will stay behind and play with Bexley," Tobin said with a wicked grin.

Waverley returned just as they were leaving.

"According to my man, Bexley is already married. Apparently, one of the fathers in Spain held him at gunpoint."

"There is no chance, then, of him giving her the protection of his name," Thackeray said.

"That is irony if ever I heard it," Philip drawled.

"Have you found a record of it?" James asked, considering all the options as they made their way back to Hyde Park.

"No, but we questioned everyone in his regiment and heard from a soldier who was there. I still think it worth having him sign something. How likely is it a marriage in Spain is legal? It would have been

Catholic. Regardless of that, I doubt if the truth of anything will come out until long after Bexley is gone."

James was not sure if having Bexley's name would be better or worse for Fenella. If Waverley had discovered Bexley was married, then surely someone else could do so?

"I am still thinking it would be better for her to have a marriage certificate in case she should need it," Waverley said. "It took a significant amount of digging to find a whisper of the other marriage, and there is apparently no proof."

"There are no titles to convey if she is with child, but at least the child would not be labelled a bastard," Philip agreed.

"No, but his mother would be a bigamist," Tobin, ever the sarcastic pessimist, pointed out.

"She need not know," Waverley retorted.

James had to stop the madness. "Gentlemen. We must find her and discover what has occurred before we arrange the rest of her life." All James cared about was finding Fenella safe, and returning her to her family.

"I have directed the men to search the rooms in Covent Garden they believe are his."

"I expect he had already abandoned those and was about to flee," Tobin put in.

"Let us return to the Park, then. The idea has a great deal of merit," Matthias remarked.

"Did he say something to make you think she was here?" James asked Philip as they crossed the street back to Hyde Park Corner. There were still a few people about, mostly tradesmen and shop-keepers on their way home, but thankfully the fashionable elite had departed to prepare for the evening's revelries.

"It was a strong feeling I had. He seemed surprised by the situation. I do not think he realized he had been tricked until they were already there."

"That does surprise me," James admitted. "Should we separate to look for her? Each of us take a corner and work our way around it and fire a single shot in the air if we discover her. We can avoid the wide-open areas."

"I wish I had thought to desire the guardsmen to remain behind. My men are still searching Covent Garden, but will report to Waverley Place when they have finished. There is naught for it; the four of us it will have to be. Very well, we will proceed with your plan as best we may. I was thinking he may have installed her at either of the keeper's cottages or in the trees on the far side from here," Waverley suggested.

"I think one person can take from here directly to the other side, if moving briskly. Between here and the lake and the parade grounds, there are not too many hiding places beyond the water, the woods are much thicker," Phillip added.

Matthias volunteered to look over the closest area, because he could not ride as fast. He could also stop and question people to discover if either Fenella or Bexley had been seen. Philip decided to ride along the southern edge of the lake and back along Rotten Row.

James and Waverley rode to the northern side, then spread out, uniformly to cross together in parallel lines across the remaining portion toward Kensington Gardens. They would then all meet back at the Cheesecake House.

James hoped Philip's intuition was correct, because he could only imagine where Fenella might be otherwise. He did not think for a moment that Bexley had planned to leave with her. She was far too young and silly for someone like him. He would certainly have used her for his own means and planned to dispose of her as soon as possible.

They were not long into their search before one of Waverley's men waved to them from a sweating horse.

"Have you news, Geordie?"

"Yes, your Grace. We were finally able to search the rooms where Bexley had been staying, but the place was turned out earlier today."

"You are certain he was there?"

"Yes. He also had in keeping with him a red-headed young woman who had a ladylike way about her. The landlord was quite angry when he realized he had left without paying this week's rent. I gave him enough to open his budget and then he told me everything he knew."

"Excellent. Did he have any idea where they might have gone?"

"Somewhere on the Continent, was the landlord's understanding. Bexley was talking about his soldiering all the time. 'We don't get too many the likes o' him hereabouts,'" he said.

"I would have thought Bexley would have wished to remain unobtrusive," the Duke murmured. James suspected he was annoyed they had not found Bexley sooner. "Well, she must be somewhere near at hand. We had better carry on, then." He stopped. "Geordie, take some men and search the docks, just to be certain."

"Yes, your Grace."

Methodically, they looked behind every tree and crossed back and forth so as not to miss anywhere. By the time they had gathered near the western edge and were heading towards the Cheesecake House, it was growing near to dusk.

"I do not think she is here. They will close the gates soon," Philip said, approaching them on his black mount.

James hated to return to Anna without her sister. "Has anyone any more suggestions? Should we search outside the Park's boundary? Mayhap between here and the Gardens, if that is where he came from?"

Philip shook his head. "I still do not think she can be far off."

"But where could he have left her, restrained, without making a spectacle?"

Waverley slid from his horse and tied it to a post near the bridge leading to the Cheesecake House. "I need some refreshment before we search any further.

"I doubt this place is still open," James said doubtfully, but of course, almost anywhere would be open to Waverley.

James had not even thought about food or drink, but now that he did think of it, he was rather parched. He joined the Duke, and the others followed, Matthias noticeably limping. Perhaps it was time to call a halt for the night.

They entered the small tea room, which was indeed closing, only to see Fenella sitting alone in the corner. "Oh, there you are, James!" she cried gaily. "But where is Bexley?"

HOW MUCH LONGER WOULD IT be before there was any news? Annag was trying hard not to panic, but she knew something must be wrong. If Bexley had cooperated, Fenella would already be home. Her mother had been sent to bed with laudanum to calm her nerves, and her father had sought refuge in his study. Annag was left to pace about and wonder and wait, imagining the worst, while trying to ignore the pain in her arm. She went back to the front window of the drawing room for what must have been the thousandth time. She had even drunk several cups of tea while standing there at the window and feeling helpless. Dusk was beginning to fall, and Annag did not know what else to do. Would they keep searching all night? She wished someone would at least bring her some tidings.

It was half past nine when she finally saw a group of riders approaching the house. She ran to the front door and out to the steps, frantic for news. That was when she saw her sister, riding before James on a bay gelding.

"Fenella!" she exclaimed with relief. Fenella slid down from the horse, and Annag embraced her as fiercely as she could with her injured arm.

"La, Annag! You are crushing my bones!"

"Forgive me, but you cannot know how worried we have been."

"I sent a letter to Mama, explaining everything," the girl said carelessly as she walked on into the house, not even remarking upon Annag's injury. Annag met James' gaze as he handed his horse to a groom who had come scurrying. James shook his head, then came to her.

"We found her waiting for Bexley in the Park," he explained briefly. "She still thought they were to run away together once he had the funds."

"And where is he?" Annag asked, both embarrassed and incredulous at her sister's wild behaviour.

"Still at Headquarters. He has told us nothing. We found her on our own."

The Duke spoke from his horse. "We will return to Horse Guards now. If Lady Fenella happens to mention anything which might assist the investigation, please send word."

"Of course," James replied before Annag could do so. Placing a hand on her back, he guided her into the house.

She stopped at the door.

"What is it?" he asked.

"I need a moment to compose myself. The urge to strangle my sister is very strong at this moment."

"I fully sympathize, my dear. When I found her sitting waiting at the tea shop, looking for all the world as though she were annoyed that we were rescuing her instead of Bexley come to carry her off, you must know I showed the self-control of a saint."

"Thank you for bringing her back, nonetheless. I am not certain I would not have thrown her in the Serpentine."

Annag went through the entrance hall and into the drawing room, where Fenella was already being served tea.

"I have had nothing but tea all day. I have been sitting waiting for hours!" she said, with a long-suffering sigh.

Annag and James passed the butler as they entered. "Has my father been informed of my sister's arrival?" she asked the man.

"I will do so now, my lady."

Trying to control the anger flowing through her veins Annag sat down on a spindle-legged chair across from her sister, who was seated on a sofa, looking grumpy. The stupid girl still did not comprehend what she had done to herself and her family. She was composing a scathing set down when her father burst into the room.

"Well, daughter, what have you to say for yourself?"

"Where is Bexley? I want to see him now!" She had the gall to stamp her foot.

"You will see him, indeed you will. You will be married before he is transported—if he is not drawn and quartered first! Then we shall be away to Kiernan as soon as the carriage is ready."

"I will not go back to Scotland. I will be a married lady, and you will not be able to force me." Her petulance knew no bounds, it seemed.

Annag shook her head. "First of all, do you not realize what torture you have subjected your family to? Two weeks passed before anyone heard from you. People were searching for you all over England and Scotland!"

Fenella pursed her lips. "Bexley said he would send my letter the next day. How was I to know it would take two weeks to reach you?"

"Why did you do such a thing in the first instance?" Throwing up her free hand, Annag rose and began to pace about the room, her agitation too strong to be controlled, but James stopped her and steadied her.

"Bexley has duped many young ladies in this way, Fenella," James said, his voice irritatingly calm. Annag's was shaking.

Fenella waved her hand in a dismissive gesture. "He did not care for them. Those dalliances happened when he was a young officer. All the subalterns did such things, he told me."

"No, my lady. I served with him. He has quite a history. However, the Duke is seeking the assistance of the Archbishop, and as soon as may be, you will be married—before Bexley is punished."

"Perhaps it would be punishment enough to be saddled with you!" Annag's father said ungraciously, but she had had the same thought.

Fenella scowled.

"Did you know how much he demanded, in exchange for returning you?"

"I do not believe you." She crossed her arms and turned away.

"Fifteen thousand pounds, Fenella! He had no intention of taking you with him! When will you get it into your silly head that what you do affects others? Do you know how indebted we are to people I scarcely know? Do you comprehend how hard it has been, attempting to protect our family's name? What of Innis? If this gets out, she will have no chance of a respectable marriage. We will return to Scotland, holding our heads in shame. It is no more than you deserve, but that your mother and sisters should be served such a turn is unforgivable."

"I want Bexley," Fenella insisted.

"You selfish, selfish jade! You are no better than a harlot!"

Annag began to fear her father really would have a heart seizure. His face was red, and his veins were pulsing in his neck. She went to him. "Perhaps it might be for the best if you were to rest now, Papa."

"Not until I have seen her married." He turned to her sister. "You will be locked in your bedchamber until then. Perhaps I will beg them to transport you on the boat with him!"

"I would prefer that to returning to Scotland!"

Taking Fenella's arm, their father hauled her to her feet and then dragged her, protesting, from the room.

After closing the door behind them, James went to pour a drink. Annag was too astonished for words to pass her lips. James placed a drink in her hand, then placing his own about them, carried the glass to her lips. The warm fire slid down her throat, and did relax her enough to soothe her trembling. "I am sorry you had to witness that. Was it too much to hope for remorse, at the very least?" she asked, not expecting an answer. "I do not know why I should be surprised. And all the while I have been imagining her frightened to death."

James put a soothing hand on her back and rubbed in gentle circles, but still said nothing. His quiet was disconcerting. He must be glad of his escape from this family, she thought bitterly.

"What will happen now?" she asked.

"As your father said, Waverley is trying to convince his uncle, the Archbishop, to marry them. Then he will be sentenced, perhaps sent to Australia—if he is fortunate."

She sagged against him with relief. "I was so afraid you would call him out."

"Bexley is no gentlemen. No one in their right senses would choose to duel with him."

"I still cannot believe she sat in the Cheesecake House in the Park all this time, waiting for him. I do not think Fenella has ever been so obedient in her life!"

"You are no more shocked than we," James said, leading her to the settee. "We were about to give up for the night when we saw her sitting, as calm as you please, in the corner."

"And of course, instead of being grateful, she becomes angry. She does not deserve such consideration, James."

"No, but you do. We should have dealt with him long ago."

"You cannot blame yourselves. Fenella would have found a way to ruin herself. If not Bexley, it would have been someone else, I am quite sure."

"Perhaps. Will you be well enough if I leave you now? I should join the others. It is clear that Fenella will not offer anything against him."

"No, she is quite deluded. Do not concern yourself on my behalf, I shall retire. If it can be arranged for her to go with him, I think it might be for the best. My parents should not have to suffer whatever scheme she will concoct if she is left on these shores without him."

"I will do what I may." James kissed her on the head and withdrew, leaving her feeling desolate rather than relieved.

CHAPTER 20

*B*exley should have negotiated when he had the chance," Philip remarked. They had gathered for a drink at Waverley Place after leaving Bexley in a cell for the night.

"I am rather glad he did not," James said. "It is satisfying to see him get his just desserts for once."

"Poor Lady Fenella. I am not certain she understands precisely what she is in for," Waverley reflected.

James was glad his friends had not been privy to her outburst earlier or they might think Lady Fenella was perhaps getting what she deserved—but that was an uncharitable thought that he would never speak aloud.

"Frankly, I think India is too good for him." Tobin sneered into his glass. "I do not think Prinny would have been so gracious had it not been for Lady Fenella wishing to accompany the blackguard. Perhaps you may still change her mind?" Tobin asked with a hopeful look. "I would very much like to watch him be drawn and quartered. I would also like to be riding one of the horses at the time," he said with a wicked grin.

"One for each of us," Philip agreed as he raised his glass. "Do you think Prinny might be prevailed upon to reinstate the practice?"

"At least allow Lady Fenella to have the marriage license that she may be widowed instead of ruined," Thackeray added.

"I must thank you all for your assistance," James interposed. "I know Lady Calder and Laird McKiernan consider themselves deeply indebted to you." He raised his glass again to toast his friends.

"We all know why we took part in the adventure, though I would like to think we might have done so even had another poor young lady been involved. By tomorrow morning, it will be at an end." Waverley looked relieved.

"Not quite," Thackeray pointed out. "Bexley's capture was not a completely private matter. There could still be consequences."

"No, but the details were not public knowledge. Hopefully, with the marriage and the new position in India, people will assume the matter to be more trivial than they had doubtless hoped."

"Waverley dictates, therefore it shall be so," Philip teased.

They laughed, then moved on to reminiscing about other times.

"We must make a point of gathering more often, for no other purpose than visiting," Waverley continued. "Shall we gather for Christmas this year?"

"The weather and the Irish Sea permitting, and pending Bridget's approval," Tobin said with a knowing grin.

"Then the matter is settled." The Duke had once again decreed, but they did not remind him this time.

"Will you be bringing Lady Calder?" Philip asked James with a sly smile.

"You know very well that I cannot support such a one as she. That was made very clear to me ten years ago, and that was why I found myself a lieutenant without a beard on a ship to the Peninsula."

"Is that why you sport such a horrendous one now?" Tobin teased.

"Spoken by the one who still has none," James retorted, to guffaws of laughter.

"I do not think the lady minds," Philip remarked, once they had stopped laughing. "We have all seen the way she looks at you. And you know that there is plenty of opportunity awaiting you, should you wish it."

"I am a farmer now, if you recall."

"I do believe Barrett would be quite content to remain at Alchnanny, should a certain sister decide to forgo her attempt to make a coup amongst the *ton* and thereby catch herself one of the most eligible *partis*," Waverley pointed out.

"I want only Margo's happiness. I will speak to her about it."

"And I can vouch for Barrett's worthiness if you had not already surmised that for yourself."

"Lady Calder will wish to be near her son…" James paused and stared at his friends. "I cannot believe I am even entertaining the idea." He shook his head and swirled the amber liquid in his glass.

Tobin spoke up. "I can also vouch for the worthiness of Waverley's enterprise. I had little to invest in the beginning, but now have a tidy fortune."

"You already have a stake in it, James. I formed it that way, and everyone was given an equal part. Those who invested more now have a larger share, of course, but you still have a healthy sum, nonetheless. I will have my overseer speak with you about it, if you wish. Then you may make your own decision without my interference."

They all laughed. As though Waverley could help but interfere.

As James went to bed that night, he had a great deal on his mind. The thought of never seeing Anna again weighed heavily on his heart. Could he make her truly happy? Would she want to be married to a man who made his livelihood in trade? Yes, while the others were involved in the same enterprise, they were also secure behind their titles, except for Philip. He and Lady Amelia seemed very happy. Perhaps Anna would be happier were she out from under the Dowager's thumb. The only way to know would be to ask her.

Yet still he hesitated. She had a son. Perhaps it would not cause any difficulty, but Anna had said he needed a man's guidance. What if the boy wanted nothing to do with him? What if the young Earl's trustees did not approve of a poor farmer—ex-soldier—new businessman— being a stepfather? Anna had been afraid of the boy's uncle; would their marriage be ammunition the man could use to keep the boy from her?

James could never allow himself to come between mother and son. Did Anna not realize their marriage could be more harmful than helpful? Very likely not, he reflected. She did not know how deep such prejudices tended to run. James had a feeling it would take all the power possessed by the brethren to bring about a satisfactory conclusion. It was not a comforting thought to know he was not acceptable in his own right, but he had learned that lesson long ago. He was foolish for even thinking of marriage, and yet he also could not imagine the future without her.

THE ARCHBISHOP WAS none too pleased to perform a ceremony he thought was circumspect at best. However, once he was assured the couple would no longer be living anywhere in Europe, and that Bexley had denied a previous marriage, he was more willing to accede. He expressed, in severe tones, the hope that marriage would settle Bexley into a more orderly manner of conduct and protect Lady Fenella's name. James had no such delusions. Bexley would no doubt be a scoundrel wherever he went, and Fenella... well, she had chosen her path.

All of the brethren, and their wives, attended the wedding, but other than Anna's family, that was the sum total of guests. None of them wanted Bexley to have a chance of escape. As soon as the wedding had ended, Philip and Tobin were to escort the couple to the docks, where they would be guarded until the ship sailed.

James felt fear intrude as decisions had to be made. Even though the ceremony was a mere formality of reciting the vows, he felt many emotions roil within him. He detested Bexley and was jealous of him at the same time. Why he should feel that way, James could not say. Perhaps because he was wishing for the married state himself? Of course, a marriage between Bexley and Fenella would not be an easy one. James shook his head as he watched the ceremony, Lady Fenella looking delighted as though she had not just subjected her family to two weeks of torment—not to mention what he and the brethren had done. Who knew what would have happened to her or her family had the latter not had connections with them and the resources to which they had access?

The ceremony ended, and the register was signed. They all heaved a collective sigh of relief. Fenella was permitted to beam and pronounce herself fortunate to have married in her first Season. Barely suppressed glances of understanding passed between the brethren.

To those who watched, it appeared to be a quaint Society wedding at St. George's, Hanover Square, but Bexley and Fenella had a heavy guard as they left the church and climbed into the waiting carriage.

The brethren waved them on their way, Philip and Tobin riding behind, and then stood for a while under the portico, Anna speaking with her parents and the Duke and Duchess.

James determined to speak with her before it was time to leave, but first, he must deal with his own personal affairs.

He did not wish to answer the questions she might well ask until he knew his own mind. His heart was already decided.

"You will not let her go, will you?" Thackeray spoke in his ear. Nearby, Kitty was speaking with Lady Amelia and Bridget.

"I do not want to," James admitted, "but I must ensure that accepting my hand will be best for her and her son."

"Allow the lady the choice," Matthias suggested. He gave him a pat on the back, and turned to answer a question his wife was asking.

James looked up and caught Anna's gaze, whereupon she began to make her way towards them, passing by the Duke and Duchess who were standing nearby.

"Will you do me the kindness of one favour before you return to Scotland?" she asked. James did not know what to think. Had he misjudged her feelings? Had she decided she did not want him after all?

"Of course," he answered, trying hard not to wear his heart on his sleeve.

"Would you mind horribly, escorting me to Eton and spending the holiday with Tommy and myself?"

It was not at all what James had expected. She had mentioned wanting him to stand in place of a father, but this was not how he had imagined it happening.

"You need not answer yet. I can see you are surprised. We would not be able to go to one of his properties, of course, but I thought a trip to the sea would be lovely. I have never been to the southern shores."

"Supposing his trustees were to find out? Are you prepared for the worst?"

"Do you mean, to marry you?" She looked amused. "Of course. But are you?"

James looked up and Waverley was grinning at him. Had he over-heard? It seemed as though James' decision would be taken out of his hands.

ANNAG KNEW James was struggling with his response to her proposal, and therefore was not surprised when he did not call the next day.

She began to make the necessary arrangements to pick up Tommy from school and remove to Runnymeade, although she knew life there alone would be desolate and depressing. She must carry on. There was nothing else she could say or do to convince James, short of setting propriety on its head and asking *him* to marry *her*, though she had in a way. While it would break her heart, she would leave, knowing she had done everything she could. Perhaps, she mused, asking him to holiday secretly with Tommy and her had been a mistake. It was wrong, and maybe she had pushed him too far.

She instructed her maid to pack her trunks. Thankfully, she had been able to acquire a few new gowns while in London, and would no longer be confined to drab colours. It was a new beginning.

There was one more day before she had to leave. It was hard not to hold out hope that he would come. Her parents were also to leave for Scotland, as the Season was drawing to a close anyway. Hopefully, if there was any scandal, no one would remember by next year, and Innis could begin again. Her sister had attracted some few suitors, and

Annag would see to it that Innis did not suffer from Fenella's misdeeds. Annag would even come to London again, should it prove necessary. Perhaps it would be a happy notion to invite Innis to spend part of the year with her so she did not become too lonely. She would try not to dwell on James. Before, when she married and missed him beyond belief, she had managed to shut away her emotions and survive. She could do it again.

"Annag, will you walk in the park with me?" Innis asked, standing in the doorway to her apartments.

Annag turned. "I did not see you there. Yes, some fresh air would be welcome. I am feeling a little maudlin this morning. Let me fetch my bonnet."

Soon afterwards, they left the house arm in arm, and walked along Oxford Street to Hyde Park. Had it truly only been two days since that horrible scene with Bexley? It still seemed too fantastic an emprise to believe it had happened, yet Fenella was married and gone. In all likelihood they would never see her again. Their mother had wailed once they had returned to Calder House and reality had to be faced. It was too late for recriminations, and while Annag did not wish her sister ill, she strongly suspected Fenella also would suffer for her mistakes.

"Are you sad to leave London?" Annag asked her other sister.

"I am indeed," Innis replied. "It was difficult to enjoy myself once Fenella had disappeared. It took a lot of effort to pretend everything was normal. We were quite deceived in Major Bexley."

"Indeed, although pray do not allow him to colour your opinion of everyone. There are many good, kind gentlemen, you know."

"I hope so."

"You were not even in London for the entire Season. I will bring you back again. I should not have left you in Mother and Father's care in the first place. For all their age, they are rather naïve about Society."

"Do not feel obligated, sister. I have at least had the chance to see it. I am sure Mother and Father would be willing to take me to Edinburgh."

Innis had matured a great deal in that short time; catastrophe tended to do that.

"Look, there is Margo with Captain Frome!" Innis began to wave furiously as they walked along the path through the park.

Annag was glad, if nothing else, that her spirit was not completely dampened. She could not control the lurching of her heart when she saw him. It had ever been thus.

Now, however, it was difficult not to feel pain too, knowing she was about to lose him all over again. Somehow she knew this time would be much worse, because this time he would be choosing to leave her.

"Good afternoon, ladies." He made a polite bow.

Innis had already released Annag's arm and taken Margo's. They were walking towards the Serpentine with their heads together, chatting furiously. Annag watched them, glad that they still had each other through this unfortunate episode.

Slowly, she turned back towards James, trying to fight the thickening of her throat. She very much wanted to cry. She did not know what to say to him, but having taken a deep breath, she spoke anyway.

"Well, James, this would seem to be where we make an end. I was wondering if we would have a chance to say goodbye."

"That would be a shame," he said, taking her arm and beginning to walk along behind their sisters.

"It would be a shame," she agreed.

"Forgive me if I presume too much, but I have arranged to take you and Tommy to Waverley's summer estate. I know you longed for the beach, but this way we would be close to Tommy's school and under the chaperonage of the Duke and Duchess. Shall I refuse the invitation?"

Had she heard him correctly? She stopped and looked up to search his face. He was grinning down at her.

"Do you mean it?"

"I would not tease you after all you have suffered. However, I do not wish to make any more decisions until I discover whether or not Tommy will be able to care for me."

"How could he not? Oh, James! You have made me very happy. I had thought I might never see you again."

"Silly girl."

"Mayhap, but you cannot blame me for fearing the worst, when that seems to have been the way of things before now."

"There is one matter, however, if we are to marry."

"What is that?" Annag's heart leapt with happiness. That abused organ was not wise enough to heed the caution in his words.

"We cannot live on your son's fortune. We will need to find somewhere else to live."

"Will you not return to Alchnanny?" What was he saying?

"Would you be very upset if I did not? It is not necessary. It seems Mr. Barrett and Margo have eyes only for each other. I spoke with her this morning, and while she enjoyed her stay here, she does not wish to live amongst the *ton*. It seems that the opportunity to become a lady and have great wealth matters not to her."

Annag smiled. "I can sympathize with that. If her heart is set on Mr. Barrett, then I wish them well. They are happy to run the estate, I gather?"

"Indeed. He has offered to purchase it from me. I can see no reason why I must keep it for myself since I have no head for farming. It will stay within the family, and I will make him a very fair offer in exchange for Margo's lack of dowry."

"I am quite certain that to him Margo is a prize herself."

"That is precisely what he said. I marvel he has the means to purchase the farm at all."

"The Duke seems very fond of him and his father. What, then, will you do to occupy yourself? I know you did not relish the idea of farming, but you would have done it."

"It seems I am to be in trade. Will that offend you?"

"I cannot understand why it is so shameful to work. I think there are many gentlemen who make investments, which is no different. I know even Calder did."

James patted her arm. "This will be in partnership with my brethren, under an enterprise that Waverley began when he sold his commission."

"If the cap fits the Duke's head, why not yours?"

"I do not have the title of duke to hide behind, Anna."

"Are you certain we cannot live at one of Tommy's properties?" she asked. "There are numerous estates that otherwise sit empty. I see nothing wrong in our being caretakers of one of his properties in exchange for a place to live."

"I cannot imagine his trustees would find favour with such an arrangement. It is not merely my pride speaking, Anna."

She shook her head. "As I have said before, I do not need luxuries. I hope our journey here has convinced you of that fact. I would be happy in a small hut, were I with you."

"Let us hope it will not come to that." His eyes were twinkling as he spoke.

"Then your decision rests on whether or not my son approves of you? I appreciate the sentiment, but it may take time. How long will you make me wait, James?"

"I intend to woo him with his favourite things," he said with a mischievous grin. "If he cannot like me after that, then I do not believe there will be any possibility at all."

She smacked him lightly with the back of her hand, still very much aware that they were in public, but the light-hearted teasing filled her with so much hope she could barely contain her happiness. On the morrow, she would see Tommy again, and the three of them would be together as a family.

CHAPTER 21

*J*ames was nervous. He could only recall feeling thus a couple of times: when he had gone to ask Laird McKiernan for Anna's hand, and before his first battle. Why was meeting an eight-year-old boy equally daunting? It ought to be simple, but James knew better. After all, they could do as they pleased, and tell Tommy later, but that was not how James wished to begin a lifelong relationship.

If someone had told James, when he left Belgium, that this was how his future would look, he would not have believed them. He could not have seen how any of this could be possible, and yet here he was. His debts were on their way to being paid, his parents were settled, one sister was married, and another soon would be, while also farming the estate James did not want. What had he done to deserve such fortune? And Anna—beautiful, wonderful, constant Anna.

If there was one piece of this situation that made the least sense, it was how she could choose him. Yet it seemed, somehow, they were meant to be together after all—if Tommy consented, that was.

He had been ready since cock crow and arrived at Calder House before the household was fully awake. Thus they set off early that morning in Anna's carriage. Nervous excitement, it seemed, had affected both of them. It was decided that James would only accompany her as far as Waverley's Morningside estate, then she would go on alone to meet Tommy. James thought it would be better for them to have a little time alone before the boy found himself presented with a new papa.

Now, as James waited for them to return, he could not sit still.

"You are going to wear a hole in my rare and expensive carpets," Waverley said with amusement. "Would you care for another ride?"

"We have already ridden for most of the morning," James said with a shake of his head. "Besides, they should be here soon, and I would miss their arrival."

"Tommy will like you, James. You are good with children. I am not certain Francis does not prefer you to me," he said wryly.

"Frances likes everybody," James retorted, "but that is beside the point. She is not Tommy."

"I hear a carriage now." Waverley inclined as head towards the door.

James took himself from the study and down the hall to the entrance. The footman barely had time to scramble to the fine walnut door to open it before James did.

"There is naught quite like appearing eager," Waverley remarked from behind them. "Would you apprise her Grace our guests have arrived and to bring Frances down to greet them?" the Duke said to the butler. James scarcely heard, for he was intent on watching the approaching carriage.

When it arrived and halted in the gravelled sweep before the grand mansion, he dashed to open the door and handed Anna down, one arm still in a sling. Under cover of shaking out her skirts, she squeezed his arm. She was smiling, which was a good sign.

Tommy appeared in the doorway behind her. He was smaller than James had expected, but anyone looked small next to him, he supposed.

"Tommy, this is Captain Frome who I have been telling you about," Anna explained to her son.

James put out a hand to help him from the carriage, and Tommy accepted the help. James did not know why he had expected rejection, but he was relieved. The boy looked much like Anna, except for his dark hair. That was also a relief, James mused, to know he would not be constantly reminded of the elder Calder—the one who had taken his place.

"Welcome to Morningside, Lord Calder," Waverley said in greeting.

Tommy made a very proper bow in response. "Thank you, your Grace."

The Duchess came out, holding Francis, and also welcomed Tommy to their summer residence. "Shall we go inside? I hear Cook has made ginger biscuits."

"Thank you, your Grace." He turned to James. "Then may I see your horse?" he asked.

James threw a surprised glance at Anna. "I told him all about Sancho and Morag's adventures," she explained.

"Is it true that he understands what you are saying?"

"Oh, yes. He is very impudent. Would you perhaps like to ride him?"

"Oh, could I, sir? I have never been allowed on anything bigger than a pony."

"Then I think it only fitting that Sancho be your first big horse. He is a war-horse, but he can be gentle when he wishes."

James would threaten his beast's life, but he did not think it was necessary.

"Mama said you were a soldier. Were you at the battle they call Waterloo?" he asked with awe.

"I was."

"I want to be a cavalryman when I grow up."

"I hope we are done with war for a very long time," James said, "but you must be an excellent horseman first."

"Yes, sir." A pair of eager blue eyes looked up at him.

Anna cleared her throat in gentle reproof, though it was hard to do. "Do not forget your manners, Tommy. Her Grace made you an invitation. Shall we go in and eat those biscuits? We may visit Sancho later."

"I do beg your pardon, your Grace," Tommy apologized politely and immediately went into the house with the Duchess.

"It seems a good start," Anna said, as she again took James' arm and they walked up the marble steps together.

"What did you say about me?"

"I told him the truth—that I was considering remarrying, and that I had wanted to marry you before you went away to war."

James stopped and looked down at her. "And how did he take that?"

"Surprisingly well. He asked if you were to be his new papa."

"And you told him what?"

"I told him the truth, of course—that you wanted first to be sure he approved of you."

There was nothing like pressure to set a fellow on his mettle!

"Just be yourself, and he will love you. He already sees you as a figure of hero-worship."

"The hero-worship is for what he thinks I am. The truth may be far more disappointing."

She laughed. "I have no worries on that account."

Tommy consumed his biscuits in what must have been record time.

"May we go now, sir?" he asked eagerly. James could hardly let the opportunity pass.

"Make your bow, then, sprout," he replied humorously.

"May I come too?" Anna asked. "Or would you rather be alone, just you gentlemen?"

Tommy moved towards his mother and asked in a quiet voice, "Would you mind very much if we go alone, Mama? I promise to spend time with you later, but there is something I need to speak with Captain Frome about."

"Of course. Enjoy your ride." James glanced at Anna over Tommy's head, giving her an intrigued look.

James could tell that it was difficult for the boy to control his excitement. He would almost skip to the stables and then stop himself and try to walk with more decorum.

James had purposely not sent ahead to the stables for Sancho, because he thought it would be better for the two of them to spend the time required to brush and saddle the horse in becoming acquainted.

"Lord Calder, I should like you to meet Sancho. Sancho, this is Lady Calder's son, Tommy. We have talked about Tommy, remember?" Sancho gave him an impertinent look and then turned to nuzzle Tommy, which made him giggle.

"We are going to brush and curry him, then put his saddle and bridle on him. Have you ever done that?"

"Yes, sir. The head groom at Radford taught me how to care for my pony."

James nodded with approval and handed the boy a brush.

Sancho cooperated beautifully, and James waited for the boy to say what he needed to say. James had overheard the words Tommy had spoken to his mother earlier.

Still the boy said nothing, however, so James thought he would begin. "How are you liking school?"

"I do not mind it, sir," the boy said, looking down.

"Do you miss your mama?" James slid the saddle into place on Sancho's back, fastened the girth and adjusted the stirrups.

Tommy nodded. "She was very sad when I left Radford. I did not want to leave her there alone. Grandmother is not nice to her."

"I know she misses you, but I know she also wants you to be happy."

"She was not happy with my father."

James' hands stopped what they were doing, and he looked down at the boy. How did he know such a thing? Surely Anna would not have said so?

"He hardly ever came home," the boy continued.

"I am sorry, Tommy." James squatted down on his haunches to be eye to eye with him.

"My mama wants to marry you, she told me. She said you would be different."

"I could not imagine living my life separated from either of you," James told him, and was surprised how much he meant it. "Would you object to having me for a papa, Tommy? I would never replace your father, but help you to be the gentleman he would want you to be. I know it is too soon for you to know, of course. You can answer me later, but it is true. I had intended to ask you for permission to pay my addresses."

Tommy cocked his head to one side and wrinkled his little face. "What is 'pay your addresses'?"

James laughed. "It means I was going to ask your permission to marry your mama."

"If you promise to make my mama happy, then I will say yes when you ask."

James could not hold back a wide grin. The boy was trying so hard to be mature. He began to hold out his hand for a shake, then decided to pick up the boy instead. Tommy threw his arms around James' neck, clinging fiercely. James reciprocated, then threw him up into the saddle. "Shall we take a ride, sprout?"

~

Annag watched from the drawing room as her two loves walked away down the garden path toward the stables and felt cautiously optimistic.

"I think they will do very well," the Duchess said behind her. Annag turned to see was holding Frances and swaying with her.

"I believe you are in the right of it." Annag moved from the window as her menfolk moved out of her sight. "But now I have to wait and wonder." She laughed nervously. "I have never seen James thus, I will admit."

"Serious, do you mean?" Waverley laughed.

"Well, yes. He says he must have Tommy's blessing."

"I think that is very sweet," Meg said.

"I must confess it will not be easy. My late husband's family may not be accepting of James."

"He happened to mention you saw Archibald Radford during your travels. Is he the one who troubles you?" Waverley asked.

"The Dowager is not overly fond of me, either," Annag replied with a wry look.

"What can they have to say against a land-owning war hero?"

"He is Scottish," Annag answered succinctly.

"I am certain if it came to that, I could find something with which to convince the Honourable Archibald. He is an MP."

Frances put her head on the Duchess's shoulder and began to suck her thumb. "It is time for her nap," her Grace announced. "I will return in a few minutes. I will take her up to her nurse."

"Has James told you he plans to sell Alchnanny so that Mr. Barrett may marry his sister, Margaret?" the Duke asked as Meg left.

"He has. He said he proposes to join an enterprise with you and your fellow brethren."

"The stubborn fool has always been a part of it. He has simply chosen not to participate until now. However, he is in a better position to support you than he might have led you to believe."

"I do not care for any of that," she began, a moment before the butler appeared in the doorway. Breaking off, she turned her attention back to the window. She knew it would be some time before James and Tommy returned, but she could not help but look for a glimpse of them.

"He has had the audacity to come here?" the Duke asked in a somewhat incredulous tone, causing Annag to look back and see what the fuss was about. He held a slim white card in his masculine hand.

"I have put him in the small parlour, your Grace. Should I show him up?"

Waverley looked at Annag. What do you wish, Lady Calder?" he asked.

"Who is it?" She had not been paying any attention to what the conversation, thinking it had naught to do with her.

"The very devil of whom we were just speaking."

"Archibald Radford is here?"

"Indeed. It would seem he is looking for your son."

"I do not understand. I expect I should see him."

"I can deal with him if you so wish," Waverley offered, as though he would relish the task.

"If you would have no objection to remaining in the room, I would appreciate it, but I think I should be present."

"Very well." The Duke inclined his head. "Show him up, Timmons. Annag, do try to remain calm," he advised once the servant had departed. "Even if he believes he saw you on the road from Scotland, he did not see you in company with James."

She nodded, but could not stop the trembling from within. With deep foreboding she heard the visitor's footsteps. The man who was her husband's uncle was an imposing and overbearing individual. With difficulty, Annag tried to retain some semblance of composure.

The Duchess re-entered the room from the other side, just in time for the butler to admit the man. Someone must have warned her there was a visitor. Annag was grateful for her presence.

"Mr. Archibald Radford," the butler announced.

"Waverley?" Archibald stopped short, as though surprised to find the Duke and Duchess in the drawing room.

"Were you unaware of whose house you have seen fit to visit?" the Duke asked with a mixture of scorn and amusement.

"I-I was indeed. I have followed Lady Calder from Eton; I am looking for my nephew."

"I am here, as you see, Uncle Radford." Annag curtsied to show the courtesy that he had not.

"Perhaps you would care also to greet my wife?" the Duke suggested.

Annag would have laughed had she not been so furious.

"Your Grace." Archibald made her a polished bow, though his face was reddened as if harassed.

"Now, how may we help you?"

Annag noticed he had not been offered a seat or refreshment. She hoped he was feeling like the intruder he was.

"I am come to seek Lord Calder. I was told that he left with his mother to come here."

"Has something untoward occurred? Tommy is here, but he is out riding."

"By himself?" Archibald asked pompously, as though he were looking for fault.

"He is in the company of one of my dearest friends and fellow cavalrymen, one of the finest horsemen I have ever known," Waverley answered.

"Tommy is obsessed with horses and the army, and Captain Frome was gracious enough to oblige Tommy with a ride on his war-horse." Annag hoped it would be enough to satisfy him.

"I had not known you had formed the intention of taking Lord Calder for the holiday. We were expecting to have him at Radford," Archibald sputtered.

"I am sorry for it if you were troubled, but I left explicit instructions that I would return from Scotland in time for his holiday from school. You must know I would never miss the opportunity to be with him." Annag prayed he would make no further scene. She simply wanted him to leave before James and Tommy returned.

"We had had no communication from you of late, so the Countess asked me to fetch him."

"You may inform the Dowager Countess that he is indeed with his mother," Waverley corrected with a smile, and holding out his arm, made to usher out the unwanted caller personally, and made it clear Radford would have to cause a scene to get his way.

Annag heard the clamour of someone entering the house, and prayed again that it was not Tommy and James. There was no such luck.

"Greet your uncle, Tommy," Annag said as soon as they entered the room. "He has come to make sure you are enjoying school."

Tommy made a bow. "I find school quite tolerable, sir. How do you do?"

"Very well, thank you." The man seemed taken aback by Tommy's politeness, but did not miss the chance to cast a satisfied smirk at Annag.

"Mr. Radford, may I present to you Captain Frome?"

"The famous cavalryman I have been hearing about, I infer?" Archibald said, holding out his hand. James looked amused.

Would Archibald be so courteous, Annag wondered, if he knew James and she were to marry? However, if he had decided to accept defeat and leave Tommy there, she was grateful.

The gentlemen conversed quietly while the butler brought in a tea tray. Annag had hoped the visit would be shorter than that, but she supposed it was better to maintain at least a façade of civility.

Tommy sat between his uncle and James, busily telling Archibald about Sancho the horse. He did not seem to be afraid of Archibald, who even smiled when Tommy said Sancho thought he could talk.

They took tea, and the butler entered the room again. "Lord and Lady Thackeray," he announced.

It was almost as if everyone had known, Annag thought to herself. Were all of James' powerful friends to come to lend their support? It was uncanny. They could not have known Archibald would arrive.

"We lack only Lord and Lady Kilmorgan to complete our house party," the Duke remarked. "Perhaps they will arrive soon."

"We turned around at once when we received your note," Thackeray admitted. "A house party here sounded a deal more entertaining than returning home."

"Are you acquainted with Mr. Radford?" Waverley asked as the assembled rose to greet the newcomers. "He is Lord Calder's uncle."

"It is a pleasure to meet you, sir," Thackeray said, extending his hand. "And this must be Lord Calder himself. I have heard much about you."

"Is it true you led the last charge against the cuirassiers?" Tommy asked in awe.

"Aye, and shattered my leg in the process. Who has been telling you these stories?" Thackeray asked, clearly uncomfortable with praise.

"Captain Frome, while he was letting me ride Sancho."

"Sancho let you ride him?" Thackeray asked, clearly suitably awed.

"Oh, yes, when Captain Frome asked my permission to pay his addresses to Mama," the boy said proudly.

Annag was afraid to look at Archibald. She wanted to disappear beneath the carpets.

"Tommy, you were supposed to allow me to ask your mama properly," James scolded whilst still smiling.

"Did I steal your thunder, sir?" Tommy asked with such innocence that they all laughed.

"I cannot think of a finer man to be your new papa," Waverley remarked into the awkward silence which followed.

It was just as well to have the matter brought into the light, Annag supposed. Having such support present made it difficult for Tommy's uncle to object. Would he show such restraint? Would there be consequences later?

"He said he will not replace my real papa, but will help me to be the gentleman he would have wanted." Tommy was beaming.

They all seemed to hold their collective breath as they waited to see what Archibald would do—at least Annag was. Although Waverley had brilliantly made it clear Archibald would be making an enemy of him if he objected.

"Allow me to be the first to wish you joy," Archibald said. He shook James' hand, and they both walked towards her.

"I can see I am *de trop* amongst your gathering. I do hope you will allow us to visit Tommy, though. He is all we have left of his father."

Annag was so shocked that she found it almost impossible to form words. Did they truly have his goodwill in mind? She was not so naïve as to think there would not be stumbling blocks along the way. "Of course. Tommy will want to visit with his family, and will also need to know his people and his lands."

Archibald nodded, then moved away to bid the others goodbye. Perhaps he recognized when a battle was not worth fighting.

James turned towards her. "Would it be vulgar to drop to one knee and ask you, properly, to marry me?"

"No, but it is quite unnecessary. I am so happy, James. I thought I had lost you forever."

"Well, now you have me forever."

"Do you promise?"

"My word as a gentleman, my lady. Now, may we find somewhere secluded, that I may kiss you properly?"

Annag laughed. "Before long, I promise."

There was some commotion at the door, and the butler entered, looking somewhat put out. "Lord and Lady Kilmorgan, your Grace."

"Are we late for the party?" Tobin asked.

EPILOGUE

$\mathcal{T}$he banns were called the next day so that they could be married before Tommy went back to school. To James' relief, Tommy seemed genuinely happy for the marriage. They had spent a great deal of time together, and the boy relished the attention. James was sorry the child had never really known his father, and vowed that he himself would do his best for him. Tommy had also had a great deal of attention from the brethren, all of whom he worshipped. The boy would have their support for life. James was still surprised that the uncle had given his approval, and had returned for the wedding with the Dowager Countess in tow. They now sat in a pew opposite his family, waiting for the ceremony to begin. In this instance, James was grateful for his powerful friends… it meant he could have Anna and Tommy forever.

He still could not believe his good fortune as they prepared to wed on the late summer day. He stood at the front of the church, waiting for his bride. His four best friends sat to one side, watching with their wives, and with a seat left for Peter and one for Colin. He did not know why God had chosen him to be a survivor, or to have this second chance with Anna, but he would not take it for granted.

When the doors opened, and he saw her standing on the threshold, more beautiful than any lady had a right to be, on the arm of her son —soon to be his son—he thought his heart might burst with happiness.

Although he scarcely heard the words of the ceremony, he was not unaffected. It was sacred to him. He was not only agreeing to wed Anna, but to be a father to her son.

The responsibility felt weightier than anything he had faced in his life thus far, but he was happier than he had ever been.

The wedding was simple and precious and in almost no time at all Anna had become Mrs. Frome. She also seemed happy.

He made a vow to keep her that way.

When they had returned to the house from the chapel, the Duke's chef had prepared a feast for them.

It seemed very strange to be celebrating his marriage, James thought, as he looked around the terrace, which had been set with tables and chairs. Flowers adorned the tables, where his closest friends and family sat in congenial conversation together. Even the Dowager Countess and Mr. Radford seemed pleased to be seated near, and speaking with, the Duke and Duchess, James mused wryly.

Waverley pushed back his chair and stood up, raising his glass. "I think it is appropriate to make a few toasts."

James held up his hand. "As long as you promise to direct all of them towards my beautiful wife, and avoid any commentary about me," he begged with chagrin.

"Well, old chap, the last of us has fallen. How can I not remark upon that?"

"If this is what it feels like to fall, then I am happy enough for it, though I am wary of being so serious."

Everyone laughed.

"You have never liked attention being directed towards you, yet your humour was what kept us going when reality was otherwise too difficult to face," Philip interjected.

"Now you have spoiled the order of my toast, James." The Duke scowled at him. "But I daresay we may raise our glasses to you first. And you will have to suffer through some seriousness. To one of the most honourable, brave, and worthy fellows I have known. I am honoured to call you brother and friend. I would trust you with my life and those of my children."

"But not your wife?" Tobin called out, teasing.

"He has his own now, thank you very much," the Duke retorted. "Now, my Lady Annag, we all know James is not worthy of you, for all that I have just listed his good qualities. None of us are worthy of the wives God has blessed us with. Nevertheless, he will try his best, and that is really all any of us can do."

"Here, here."

Philip stood up next. "Have you noticed that Waverley never leaves anything for the rest of us to say? Regardless, I wish you both the peace—not that my dearest Amelia provides me with peace—and happiness that comes with enduring love." He winked at his wife.

"Do not confuse this with brotherly love," Tobin added.

"Why do you not go next, Kilmorgan, since you seem inclined to correct all of us," Phillip said as he took his seat.

"That comes from years of being Waverley's batman," James teased to roars of laughter from the brethren.

"Very well," Tobin said in his deepest Irish brogue as he got to his feet, holding his glass and adjusting his coat. "My lady, the truth of it is I have never considered myself one of them, not with my humble origins. However, that mattered not a jot to the brethren, and they treated me as one of their own, even when it would have been easier to have buried me in Belgium." Pausing, he then added, with his roguish smile to each of them, "I would give my life for any of them, and now, their ladies. Welcome to the family, Lady Annag."

"Here, here." Raising their glasses, they toasted James and his bride and then drank.

Matthias stood. "It seems I must now follow the three of them. What is left to say? I too would have been buried in Belgium, were it not for these gentlemen and their wives. It is a very exclusive club you are joining, Lady Annag, but I can think of no one better for James."

"Thank you," Anna said, blushing.

They drank again, and by now their glasses were empty.

James noticed Tommy stand up beside him. He cleared his throat, and tapped his glass, so the others would allow the boy to speak. Waverley noticed, and signalled for the glasses to be refilled.

"I would also like to make a toast," he said, standing tall and speaking for all the world as if he were five and twenty instead of eight.

"I feel as though I am dreaming, and someone will soon wake me up. I did not know my father well, but I think he would be pleased to know that Captain Frome is going to be my new papa."

James saw Anna wipe tears from her face, and he took her hand and held it tightly. If the boy said much more, James would be a watering pot himself.

"I thank you, sir, for being willing to be my papa, and I know my mama loves you and that you will be good to her."

James could not stomach any more. He grabbed the boy into a fierce hug. He was not the only one wiping away tears.

"Thank you, Tommy. I will do my best by you and your mama, always."

"And Sancho said you will save his colt for me," Tommy added with a mischievous grin as he looked up at James.

James shook his head. "I have no doubt he did."

Anna rose to join in with their hug. "I am the one who feels as if she is dreaming. When I consider what might have been, I would not trade this for the world."

AFTERWORD

Author's note: British spellings and grammar have been used in an effort to reflect what would have been done in the time period in which the novels are set. While I realize all words may not be exact, I hope you can appreciate the differences and effort made to be historically accurate while attempting to retain readability for the modern audience.

Thank you for reading *What Might Have Been*. I hope you enjoyed it. If you did, please help other readers find this book:

1. This ebook is lendable, so send it to a friend who you think might like it so she or he can discover me, too.

2. Help other people find this book by writing a review.

3. Sign up for my new releases at www.Elizabethjohnsauthor.com, so you can find out about the next book as soon as it's available.

4. Come like my Facebook page www.facebook.com/Eliza bethjohnsauthor or follow on Twitter @Ejohnsauthor or feel free to write me at elizabethjohnsauthor@gmail.com

ALSO BY ELIZABETH JOHNS

ACKNOWLEDGMENTS

There are many, many people who have contributed to making my books possible.

My family, who deals with the idiosyncrasies of a writer's life that do not fit into a 9 to 5 work day.

Dad, who reads every single version before and after anyone else— that alone qualifies him for sainthood.

Wilette and Anj, who take my visions and interpret them, making them into works of art people open in the first place.

To those friends who care about my stories enough to help me shape them before everyone else sees them.

Heather who helps me say what I mean to!

And to the readers who make all of this possible.

I am forever grateful to you all.

Printed in Great Britain
by Amazon

16309676R00133